"I don't know w [barcode: D0678565]

And he realized he meant it. One moment, it all seemed so clear to him, that he should keep his hands off her, that getting intimate with Lizzie was the kind of uncharted territory he had no right to explore.

And then the next moment, he found himself thinking that he'd go nuts if he couldn't touch her, if he couldn't find out what it would feel like to kiss her.

"So…what should we do?" Her eyes were so green right then. So wide. And her mouth was soft, perfect for kissing.

"Ethan?" Her eyes searched his face. "I—"

"Shh. Don't talk. Not right now."

"Ethan…"

He took her mouth again. He simply could not resist.

Dear Reader,

Lizzie Landry has a dream. She wants to reopen her family's lost bakery in her hometown of Midland, Texas.

Hunky Texas oilman Ethan Traub has other plans for Lizzie. And they do *not* include her leaving him to start her own business. His life has been pretty near perfect for the past five years, ever since Lizzie became his assistant—both at work and at home. She's also his best friend. And did I mention she takes such good care of all his high-maintenance girlfriends?

Ethan will do just about anything to keep Lizzie as his trusty right-hand woman. He's moving to Thunder Canyon, Montana, to open his own branch of Traub Oil Industries. And no matter what, he plans to see to it that Lizzie comes with him.

She's set on resisting him. But when Ethan turns on the Texas charm, well, even down-to-earth Lizzie can't help but start seeing her best friend and boss in a whole new light.

Happy reading, everyone!

Yours always,

Christine Rimmer

RESISTING
MR. TALL, DARK
& TEXAN

CHRISTINE RIMMER

Harlequin®

SPECIAL EDITION

Special thanks and acknowledgment to Christine Rimmer for her contribution to the MONTANA MAVERICKS: THE TEXANS ARE COMING! continuity.

Recycling programs for this product may not exist in your area.

ISBN-13: 978-0-373-65607-3

RESISTING MR. TALL, DARK & TEXAN

Copyright © 2011 by Harlequin Books S.A.

www.Harlequin.com

Printed in U.S.A.

CHRISTINE RIMMER

came to her profession the long way around. Before settling down to write about the magic of romance, she'd been everything from an actress to a salesclerk to a waitress. Now that she's finally found work that suits her perfectly, she insists she never had a problem keeping a job—she was merely gaining "life experience" for her future as a novelist. Christine is grateful not only for the joy she finds in writing, but for what waits when the day's work is through: a man she loves, who loves her right back, and the privilege of watching their children grow and change day to day. She lives with her family in Oklahoma. Visit Christine at www.christinerimmer.com.

For Marcia Book Adirim.
Intrepid. Fun. Flexible.
And of course, so creative!

Chapter One

"Lizzie, don't do this to me. You know I can't live without you."

Instantly, Lizzie Landry felt her determination weakening. *How does he do that?* she wondered. At the same time, she found herself thinking that he really would be lost without her, and she did worry that he…

She caught herself.

Oh, come on. What was her problem here? After five years with Ethan Traub, she ought to be immune to his considerable charm and shameless flattery. And she was. Pretty much. It was only that she did hate to leave him when he needed her. Which was constantly.

But no. She had to be strong. The break had to be made.

She put on her sternest, most unwavering expression. "Ethan, you've been putting me off for months, and it's not going to work this time. We have to talk about this."

The melting look in those dark velvet eyes of his faded

as he scowled. She watched as his perfect, manly lips assumed a downward curve. "There's nothing to talk about," he grumbled. "You're coming to Montana with me. Eventually, if you're still unhappy with—"

Lizzie put up a hand. "I'm not unhappy, Ethan. It's been wonderful working for you. If I still had to work for *someone,* I would want it to be you."

"Great, then. We have no problem. You can *keep* working for me."

"No, I'm not going to do that. I want to be my own boss. That was always my goal—a goal it's time I reached. And you *know* that I'm ready to move on because I have told you so. Over and over and over again. Two weeks' notice. I think that's fair."

"Two weeks!" he blustered, rising from behind his desk. Bracing his knuckles on the desk pad, he loomed toward her, six-foot-four of killer-handsome, seriously imposing Texas male. "It's impossible. It's not going to happen. You'll need more than two weeks to find your replacement—not that you're going to be finding one right now. We're leaving on Thursday."

"Ethan, I told you. I'm *not* going to—"

"Oh, yeah." He cut her off before she could finish her sentence. "You are. For so many reasons."

Lizzie tried not to groan. "Please don't start on the reasons. I've heard them all."

"And now you're going to hear them again."

"Do I have a choice?"

"None." And he proceeded to tell her everything she already knew. How he couldn't get along without her, how it just wasn't reasonable for her to be talking about cutting out on him now. "You know I need time, Lizzie. It's not going to be easy finding another assistant as good as you are. Someone flexible as to living arrangements.

Someone smart. Someone calm and capable. But also fun to be around. Someone who can manage the office, the house—and have my back on the personal front…"

There was more in the same vein. Okay, yes. She'd been flattered the first time she heard it. But after months of trying to tell him she was ready to move on, listening to how she couldn't go was getting old.

She waited for him to wind down before reminding him, yet again, "Montana doesn't work for me. I'm a Texan, born and bred right here in Midland. And I'm staying here in Midland and opening my bakery as planned. You need to get used to that idea because you are not changing my mind. Not this time."

"Traub Oil needs you."

"Traub Oil managed fine without me for over thirty years."

"All right, then." He straightened to his full height. "*I* need you." He towered over her now because she remained in the chair on the far side of his desk. She considered rising to face him. Upright, after all, she was only a few inches shorter than he was and could almost stand head-to-head with him.

But no. She stayed in her seat. And concentrated on projecting calm determination. "You don't need me, Ethan. Not really. You're going to be fine."

He shook his head. "Lizzie, Lizzie, Lizzie…" And then, with a heavy sigh, he folded his long, hard frame back into his fat leather swivel chair. "How about a bonus? A… severance bonus. Stick with me a little longer, you walk away with more cash."

Do not ask, her sternest inner voice instructed. But money was money. She'd been flat-broke once. She never, ever wanted to go there again. "How big of a bonus?"

He named an eye-widening figure.

She let out a strangled laugh. "You're kidding."

"I am serious as a failed blowout preventer."

Okay, she was weakening now. Genuinely weakening. Plus, well, she did feel a little bad about letting him go to Montana without her. He had big plans for Montana. Maybe she ought to stick with him through that, at least....

There was a gleam in those dark eyes now. He knew he had her. "Think of it, Lizzie. You know you can always use a larger cushion. Startup costs multiply. They inevitably turn out to be more than you projected."

Okay, he had a point there. "How long would I have to stay on?"

He gave an easy shrug. "Oh, I'm thinking a few more months should do it."

"A few months—as in three?" She was the one scowling now.

His rueful smile could charm the habit off a nun. "Just think about it. That's all I'm asking. We'll discuss it more later."

"But Ethan, I—"

He made a show of eyeing his Rolex. "Whoa, look at the time...."

"Ethan—"

"I've got that meeting with Jamison in five. You should have reminded me."

"A minute more," she piped up desperately. "Let's just get this settled."

"Can't right now. Sorry."

"Ethan—"

"You have my offer. Think it over." He was already on his feet again.

"But I *have* thought it over and I—"

"Sorry. Really. Got to go." And, again, he was out the door before she could pin him down.

Lizzie slumped in the chair.

But only for a moment—and then she was drawing her shoulders back, smoothing her hair that tended to frizz, even in the relatively low humidity of West Texas. She was not giving up on this. Today, one way or another, she was going to finish giving her notice.

Put it in writing, her sterner self insisted. That way he would have no choice but to accept the inevitable.

But no. She just couldn't do that. Not to Ethan, who was not only her boss, but also a true friend, the one who had come through for her in a big way when she most needed some help and support.

She would get through to him. After all, he couldn't escape her indefinitely. Especially not given that she lived in his house. No matter how hard he tried to avoid her, he had to come home eventually.

The meeting with Roger Jamison went well, Ethan thought.

Roger would have no trouble holding down the fort while Ethan was in Montana. And later, if things went as Ethan planned, he would formally name Roger to replace him as Traub Oil Industries' chief financial officer.

After the meeting with Roger, Ethan could have returned to his corner office, but Lizzie would be there at her desk, guarding his door. And waiting to continue explaining how she was leaving him.

Forget that.

He was meeting his stepfather, Pete Wexler, for lunch at the club at noon. So he went on over there an hour early. He got a Coke and sat out on the clubhouse front patio and enjoyed the late-May sunshine.

Pete showed up a few minutes early and he grabbed Ethan in a hug. "This is great," Pete announced. "Good

to get away from the office, get a little one-on-one time."
Pete clapped Ethan on the arm as he released him. "Shall
we go on inside?" He gestured toward the wide glass doors.

Ethan led the way. They got a table with a nice view of
the golf course.

And as soon as they put in their order, Pete started telling him what he already knew. "You're leaving Thursday."

"Right."

"Your mother and I will try to get away Friday morning.
It's important to both of us, to be there for your brother's
wedding." Corey, born third in the family after Ethan,
was getting married on Saturday. Corey and his bride,
Erin, were settling down together in Thunder Canyon, a
great little mountain town not far from Bozeman. There
was already a big Traub family contingent in the Thunder Canyon area. Ethan had cousins there, and his older
brother, Dillon, the doctor of the family, had settled there,
too. Pete was still talking. He named off Ethan's remaining
siblings. "Jackson, Jason and Rose are going to make it,
too. The whole family will be there…."

Ethan sat back in his chair and listened to his stepdad
ramble on and thought about how long it had taken him
to accept Pete into the family. At least twenty years.

But eventually, Ethan, like his four brothers and his sister, had come around. How could he not? Pete was a good
man. A kind man, with a big heart. He doted on Ethan's
mom and had consistently been there for his stepchildren.

The hard fact, Ethan saw now, was that it had taken
him a couple of decades to forgive poor Pete for not being
Charles Traub. Ethan's dad had been tall and commanding,
a self-made millionaire before he was thirty—back in the
day when a million bucks actually counted for something.
He'd died on an oil rig twenty-eight years ago, when Ethan
was nine.

Pete had been there for Ethan's mom, Claudia, from the day that the accident happened. And that had stirred up the town gossip mill in a big way. Ethan and his brothers had suffered no end of bloody noses and black eyes defending their mother's honor and, by extension, Pete's. At the same time as they stood up for the man, they were all secretly suspicious of Pete's motives.

But in the end, there was no denying that Pete Wexler was a rock. He was no maverick. He liked to take things slow and steady, which, in terms of TOI, sometimes drove Ethan nuts. Still, Pete adored Ethan's mom and he'd been a fine husband to her for twenty-six years now. Last year he'd had a heart attack, which freaked them all out and made them all the more aware of how much he meant to them.

Now, Pete was fully recovered and taking better care of himself. Back around the time of his heart attack, he and Ethan's mom had talked about retiring. But not anymore. Pete was feeling great lately. And for the foreseeable future, they would be running Traub Oil Industries together, Pete as chairman of the board and Claudia as CEO.

Ethan knew they depended on him, but he was through waiting to be the boss. And he was a damn sight more adventurous about the business than either his mother or Pete would ever be. He'd dedicated his life to TOI, learned the company from the ground up. And he'd been CFO for six years now. It was enough. Exploration and development was the key for him. If he wanted bigger opportunities, he needed to create them. And thus, the trip to Montana.

Their food came. They dug in.

And that was when Pete brought up the resort. "About this Thunder Canyon Resort opportunity. Your mom and I have looked over the material your brothers put together." Dillon and Corey had been pushing to get some TOI capital invested in the resort. "Do we really want to take on a failing hospitality venture at this point?"

"We wouldn't be taking it on exactly."

Pete smiled. "Sorry. Figure of speech. But you know what I mean."

"I do, Pete. And come on, I wouldn't say the resort is failing. In fact, the numbers show improvement over the past year. *And* they got McFarlane House hotels to invest. I've been in contact with Connor McFarlane, second in command at McFarlane House. He's committed to seeing the resort succeed."

"You'll get with McFarlane, face-to-face?"

"We've got a meeting set up for next week in Thunder Canyon."

"Good."

"The resort owners *have* been doing some reorganization…" Ethan waited for Pete's nod before continuing. "And they've been pulling out all the stops to broaden their market, to make the resort more accessible to a wider demographic, while not sacrificing the reputation they've built as a luxury destination."

"It's only that I see no reason to rush into anything…."

"And we won't. Sit tight," Ethan reassured him. "I'll spend more time on it, go over the books thoroughly, meet with the general manager, tour every inch of the property—all before we get down to giving a yes or a no."

Pete nodded. "I know you will." And then he started in about Ethan's plans to expand into shale oil extraction once he got to Montana. Same old yadda yadda. Extracting oil from shale was cost-prohibitive. The environmental impact wasn't good. As always, Pete reiterated all the drawbacks he'd reiterated any number of times before.

Patiently, Ethan reminded him that the higher the cost per barrel of oil, and the more depleted the oil reserves, the better it looked to be investing in oil shale. He reminded his stepdad yet again that the technology for extraction was constantly improving and TOI didn't want to end up behind the curve on this.

Eventually, Pete ran out of red flags on that subject. They finished their lunch and parted in the club parking lot, where Ethan submitted to another big hug.

"I know I tend to be a little overcautious," Pete said when he let Ethan loose. "But I want you to know that I—and your mother, too, of course—not only love you and wish we could keep you right here in Midland forever. We also realize you have to get out there and break some new ground. And we admire the hell out of you for that, son."

The smile Ethan gave his stepdad then had nothing but love in it. "Thanks, Pete. In some ways, you were always way ahead of the rest of us. It took me a while to appreciate how far ahead."

Pete was looking a little misty-eyed. "See you at the board meeting."

"Yeah, see you then."

Ethan went back to the office.

Big mistake. Lizzie was waiting.

She rose from her desk as he approached his office door, blew a strand of almost-blond hair out of her eye and tried to get his attention. "Ethan, I—"

"Not now, Lizzie. I've got important calls to make."

"But—"

"Later. Soon." He pushed open his door, went through and shut it behind him. Fast.

He spent the next few hours answering phone messages, dealing with email and clearing his desk as much as possible, because he—and Lizzie, too, whether she was willing to admit it yet—would be on their way to Thunder Canyon bright and early Thursday morning.

The board of directors meeting was happening down in the main conference room. That meant he had to leave the safety of his office and get past Lizzie again.

No problem. He waited to go until she actually had to buzz him to remind him of the meeting.

And then he flew past her desk with a "Hold any messages. I'll deal with them tomorrow."

She didn't even look up. She knew there was no chance they would be discussing unpleasant subjects again that day.

The meeting included a catered meal and was over at a little after eight. No way was he going home that early. Not with Lizzie, who was both his assistant *and* his live-in housekeeper, lying in wait for him there.

So he called a couple of friends and they went out for a beer. The bar had the Rangers game on the big screens. Ethan stayed to watch them beat the Angels five to four.

By then it was after eleven. One of his buddies invited everyone to his place for a final round. Ethan went. And he was the last to leave.

He didn't pull into the driveway of his four-thousand-square-foot house in a newer, gated subdivision until after two. All seemed quiet, only the outside lights were on. It looked to him as if Lizzie had given up on him and gone to bed.

Terrific.

Very quietly, he let himself into the utility room from the garage. Lizzie's rooms were on the ground floor, in the back, not all that far from the garage entrance, so he took extra care not to make a sound. Everything was dark and quiet and the house smelled faintly of baked goods.

His mouth watered. Cookies? No. It smelled more like… muffins. Maybe blueberry. He really loved Lizzie's blueberry muffins. In fact, he could use one right now.

Following his nose, he tiptoed down the short back hallway toward the dark kitchen.

He got one foot beyond the doorway when the kitchen lights popped on. He blinked against the sudden brightness and growled, "Lizzie, what the hell?"

"Ethan, there you are." She stood by the island, wearing a very patient expression and a robe that looked as if it might have been made from some old lady's bedspread. "I was beginning to wonder if you'd *ever* get home." The muffins were on the counter, behind her, looking all fat and golden and tempting. "This is getting ridiculous. You realize that, right?"

"Are those blueberry?"

She nodded, but she didn't step aside so he could grab one. "We need to talk." A weary sigh escaped her. "You want some coffee?"

He had that sinking feeling. She was determined to leave him. He knew that. She had a dream and she wouldn't let go of it. And he was running out of ways to avoid having to let her go. "I shouldn't have paid you so well," he grumbled. "You saved too much, too fast."

She shrugged. "You couldn't help it. You're a generous man." She looked down at her feet, which were stuck in a pair of floppy terry-cloth slippers the same old-lady blue as her robe. "You've been so good me. When my dad died...I don't know if I could have made it without you." Slowly, she lifted her head and they looked at each other.

He gave in. "Okay. Coffee."

She knew he was no fan of decaf, but coffee kept him awake when he drank it at night, so she brewed decaf anyway. That was the thing about Lizzie. She knew what he wanted—and what he needed—without his having to tell her.

He took a muffin, grabbed a napkin and sat down at the

table by the dark bow window. She used the single-cup maker, so the decaf was ready in no time. She set it down in front of him. He waited until she took the chair across the table before he broke off a hunk of the muffin and put it in his mouth.

Fat blueberries and that sweet, buttery, pale yellow muffin. How was it that Lizzie's muffins always managed to be light and substantial, both at once? Delicious. Lizzie's muffins—like her cookies and her cakes, her pies and the fat loaves of bread she baked—always made him feel good. Satisfied. Happy with the world and his place in it.

At home.

Yeah. That was it. Lizzie made him feel at home.

She said, "I've been thinking about that severance bonus you mentioned."

He ate another bite, savoring it, before he spoke. "Three months, it's yours."

She shook her head. "It's just too long."

"*Two,* then." He pulled out all the stops and put on a sad, pleading expression. "Two months. Lizzie, you've got to give me a little time…"

A little time. Who did he think he was kidding?

There was only one Lizzie. She made it possible for him to lead exactly the life he enjoyed—no commitments, no strings. He worked hard and played hard, and when he got home, there was no one there nagging him. Just the sweet smell of something baking in the oven and Lizzie offering a nightcap. Or a bedtime cup of decaf and a fat blueberry muffin.

He not only needed to keep her from quitting, but he also needed to find a way to make her see that opening a bakery was a dream best left to die a natural death. He needed her to keep working for him. And to keep being his live-in best friend.

He picked up his coffee and sipped.

Not much got by Lizzie. Now, she was studying him with pure suspicion in her eyes. "What kind of scheme are you hatching?"

He rearranged his expression, going for total harmlessness, as he set down the cup. "Montana will be fun. A change. Change is a good thing."

She made a humphing sound. "In spite of your plans for getting into oil shale, how likely is it that you're going to be building an office there?"

"Very likely." He hoped. "I have *family* there. Two brothers. Cousins. And my sister and my other brothers are making noises like they might want to settle down there, too."

"An invasion of Traubs."

"Well, I wouldn't put it that way exactly."

She snorted. "I would."

He reminded her, "And I *have* found a house there."

"You mean you had *me* find you a house there."

"That's right. And you did a great job." At least judging by the pictures she'd shown him online. Neither of them had actually been there yet. But the lease was for only six months. If he didn't like it, he'd find something else.

She was giving him that don't-kiss-up-to-me-because-I'm-not-buying-it look. He didn't care much for that look. She said, "How about this? You go, I stay. I hire and train my replacement while you're gone."

Not a chance. "Forget that." He ate another bite of the amazing muffin. "I've changed my mind."

"About?"

"I want two months out of you in Montana. Forget training your replacement. When the two months are up, I'll find my own assistant."

She wrinkled her very assertive nose. "Montana. Ugh."

"Don't knock it until you've been there. Thunder Canyon is like everyone's dream of a hometown in the mountains. And the scenery is spectacular." When she only sat there staring at him mournfully, he reminded her, "You get a giant bonus. For only two more months."

She slanted him a sideways glance. "Two months would be it. The end. You accept that?"

He didn't. So he lied. "Absolutely."

"Fine," she agreed at last. "Two months. I go with you to Montana. I get that big bonus and you find your own new assistant."

"Deal." He popped the rest of the muffin into his mouth and offered her his hand across the table. She took it and they shook.

He was careful to keep his gaze steady on hers and only to smile on the inside, to give her no clue that he was lying through his teeth. There was no way she was leaving him. He just needed more time with her to make her see the light.

Two months in Thunder Canyon should be just the ticket.

Chapter Two

Late Thursday afternoon, Ethan parked his rented SUV on Main Street in Thunder Canyon. The early-June sun shone bright and the air was crisp and clean, with a cool wind sweeping down from the mountains. In the distance, snowcapped peaks reached for the wide Montana sky.

He was thinking he would walk the three blocks to the Hitching Post, the landmark saloon/restaurant that had stood for well over a hundred years now at the corner where Main jogged north and became Thunder Canyon Road.

But then, a few doors down, he spotted his sister-in-law Erika. The pretty brunette stood peering in the window of one of the shops. Beside her was a gorgeous blonde. Ethan knew the blonde, too: Erin Castro, his brother Corey's bride-to-be.

As Ethan approached, Erin turned her back to the window. She sagged against it, hanging her head. When she spoke, Ethan heard the tightness of barely controlled tears. "I can't believe this. I talked to him *yesterday…*"

Erika peered all the harder in the wide front window. "I'm so sorry, Erin. I really don't think there's anyone in there. And all the display cases are empty."

Erin tipped her head back and let out a moan. "How can this be happening? Oh, Erika, what am I going to do now? The wedding is Saturday."

Erika turned around and leaned back against the window, next to Erin. "I can't believe he would just…vanish like that." Right then, she glanced over and saw Ethan lurking a few feet away, waiting for them to notice him. She frowned. "Ethan? Hey, I didn't know you were already in town."

He nodded. "Got in an hour ago. My assistant shooed me out of the house. She doesn't like me underfoot while she's trying to unpack—and why do I get the feeling something has gone wrong here?"

Erin let out another moan. "Because it has." She aimed a thumb over her shoulder at the sign that said Closed Indefinitely in the shop window. The shop was a bakery. *La Boulangerie* was written in flowing script across the front windows. "I came over to make my final payment on my wedding cake only to find that the baker, apparently, has skipped town."

Erika said, "She paid him two-thirds in advance. Can you believe that? This is fraud, plain and simple."

"It's a disaster, that's what it is." Erin raked her shining blond hair back off her forehead with an impatient hand. "I don't even care about the money at this point. I care that it's Thursday…." A whimper escaped her. *"Thursday."*

Erika wrapped an arm around her shoulders. "We'll figure out something. There *are* other bakeries in town."

"I can't believe it. Forty-eight hours until the wedding."

Erin's huge blue eyes swam with tears. "The whole town is coming. And. No. Cake."

Ethan never could stand to see a woman cry. Plus, as soon as he'd realized what the problem was, he had the solution. "Erin, dry those tears. And come with me, you two. My car's right there."

His brothers' women looked at him as if he was a couple sandwiches short of a picnic.

Erin sniffed. "Ethan, we're both glad to see you and we'd love to spend a little time with you. But right now we've got to find someone who can deliver a six-tier wedding cake by Saturday."

"I'm with you. I get it." He took Erin's arm and wrapped it around his. And he offered his other arm to Erika. "And believe it or not, I happen to know the best baker in Texas."

Erin remained unconvinced. "That's great, Ethan, but there's no *time* to fly someone in from Texas."

"I know. And that's not a problem. The baker in question is right here in town—whipping the house I'm renting into shape, as a matter of fact."

"Uh, he is?"

"Actually, *her* name is Lizzie. She's a genius of a baker. She's at my house and we are going there now."

Lizzie stood in the formal living room of the house she'd rented for Ethan, BlackBerry in hand, and checked off the afternoon's already-accomplished tasks.

Unpack 4 Ethan. Check.

Unpack 4 self. Check.

There was more in the same vein. But overall, the house was in pretty good shape. It had come quite nicely furnished and she'd hired Super-Spiffy Housekeeping to make the place shine. Also, the Super-Spiffy folks offered a shopping service. Lizzie jumped on that, too. As a result, the pantry and fridge were now fully stocked and ready to go.

Now, to figure out what to whip up for dinner. It would have to be something she could make up ahead and stick in the fridge, just in case Ethan wandered in later with an empty stomach. And cookies might be nice. Her mama's recipe for butter pecan sugar cookies maybe. He could never get enough of those.

Yeah, okay. She totally spoiled him and she knew it. But when she baked, she was spoiling herself, too. There was nothing like the smell of cookies in the oven. Or sourdough bread. Or a sweet fruit kuchen. Or a nice devil's food cake.

The smell of something baking always made Lizzie feel that all was right with the world. It brought back memories of her childhood, as vivid and real as if they were happening in the here and now, so many years later. Memories of the little child-size table she had in the back of the family business, the Texas Bluebell Bakery. Of her mama singing "Au clair de la lune" and "Frère Jacques" as she decorated a tall, splendid wedding cake or even asked for Lizzie's help to cut gingerbread men from dark, spicy dough. When Lizzie baked, she saw her *maman*'s heart-shaped delicate face, her pink cheeks and radiant smile. She saw her dad as a young man again, a happy man. He'd met her *maman* when he was in the army, stationed in France, and he'd loved her on sight. So he'd swept her off her tiny feet and brought her home to reign over the bakery he'd inherited from his parents. Lizzie's dad had lived for her *maman*.

And when her *maman* was gone…

Lizzie blinked and shook her head. No point in going there. She had a meal to prepare. And then she had butter-thick cookie batter to mix with toasted pecans, roll into sugared balls and flatten with the round base of a glass.

She was just turning for the kitchen when she heard the front door open.

Ethan appeared from the foyer, ushering a striking blonde and a curvy, big-eyed brunette in ahead of him. He spotted her. "Lizzie, there you are."

She laughed. "Ethan, what are you up to now?"

He put an arm across the blonde's shoulders. "Lizzie, meet Corey's beautiful bride, Erin Castro." He hooked the other arm around the brunette. "And this gorgeous creature is Erika, Dillon's wife. My brothers are such fortunate men."

Lizzie recognized the two from family photos. "Hey, great to meet you both at last."

Erin said, "Hi," kind of limply. Erika echoed the word. Both women looked a little…what? Unhappy, maybe, and worried. Especially Erin.

Lizzie gestured toward the living-room sofa and chairs. "Make yourselves comfortable. I'll brew a pot of coffee and see if there's anything sweet around here…" She turned for the kitchen.

"Coffee would be great," Ethan said. "And it's you we came to see."

She stopped, turned. "Me?"

The women shared a glance. Erin spoke. "Ethan seems to think you might be able to save me from disaster."

"Yikes. There's a disaster?"

"There certainly is. A cake disaster. I went to finalize payment on my wedding cake today and found out the baker has skipped town."

Lizzie let out a groan of sympathy. "But the wedding is Saturday, isn't it?"

Erin gave a sad little sigh. "Exactly."

Ethan said coaxingly, "And I told them that you're unbeatable in the kitchen. *And* that you're planning to leave me to open a bakery…"

Lizzie grinned, pleased. "You want me to do the wedding cake."

Erin let out a cry. "Oh, it's too much. Way too much to ask." She put her hands to her pink cheeks. "I'm so sorry we bothered you."

"Hold on, now." Ethan tried to settle her down.

But Erin would not be "settled." She turned to Erika. "We really have to get going. I need to work this problem out and I need to do it yesterday…"

Lizzie ached for the poor girl. "Hey, did I say no?"

Erin blinked. "But I… Well, could you? *Would* you?"

"I can, yes. And I would be honored. And you can relax. It's very much doable. Mostly it's going to be about getting the equipment I'll need together on the fly like this. But the cake itself is no problem."

"No problem?" Erin was shaking her head. "It's for *three hundred* people."

Lizzie couldn't bear to see the poor woman so worried. She went to her, took both her small, slim hands in her own larger ones. "Let me take this worry off your shoulders. Planning a wedding is stressful enough without your baker running off on you." The man—why was she sure it had to be a man?—should be shot.

A tear trembled in Erin's thick lashes. "Oh, if you could…"

"I can. And I will. You'll see. I won't let you down. I baked several multitiered wedding cakes when I worked in my family's bakery, before college. And I've done four more since then, for friends in Texas who had big, gorgeous weddings."

The tear escaped Erin's lashes and spilled down her cheek. She freed a hand from Lizzie's grasp to take the tissue Ethan had produced for her. "I know it's only a cake. It's not the end of the world. I shouldn't let it get to me like this…"

Erika moved in closer and wrapped an arm around Erin's shoulder. "It's all going to work out." She winked at Lizzie. "My instincts tell me that Lizzie is just what we need right now."

"Yes, I am," said Lizzie with a low laugh. "Now come on into the kitchen. I'll make the coffee and see if we have some packaged cookies around here because I haven't had time to bake anything yet. You can tell me all about the fabulous cake I'll be creating for you."

"Oh, thank you. Thank you…"

Over Erin's shoulder, Ethan caught Lizzie's eye and grinned in satisfaction. Lizzie grinned right back at him. He was pleased to have found a way to solve Erin's problem. And he knew that Lizzie loved it when he brought her a challenge.

The kitchen had a big round table positioned in a bow window very much like the one in Ethan's house in Texas. In fact, Lizzie had pretty much chosen the house because it seemed to her a slightly smaller version of his Midland home. She'd known he would feel instantly comfortable here—then again, Ethan felt comfortable wherever he was.

He went right to the table and pulled out chairs for the bride and for Erika as Lizzie got the coffee going and put some Pepperidge Farm Milano cookies on a plate. Within a few minutes, they were all munching cookies and sipping coffee.

Lizzie got out her notebook. "Okay, now, tell me all about your perfect wedding cake."

Erin knew exactly what she wanted. "It has round tiers—six tiers. And real flowers. I have a lot of colors.

So I thought if the cake itself was all white, we could put the colors in the flowers. I have mauve, red, purple, apple green, light orange and lilac…" Lizzie jotted down the colors as she ticked them off.

Erika added, "Each of her bridesmaids and matrons gets a different color."

Erin smiled at her soon-to-be sister-in-law. "Erika's dress is red."

"That will be beautiful." Lizzie started sketching. "Filling?"

"Raspberry preserves? And I want fondant on top of buttercream icing for that beautiful smooth look…"

"The porcelain look," Lizzie said. "And the fondant holds up well without refrigeration."

"Yes." Erin frowned. "I know the fondant isn't usually very tasty…"

"Mine is—does that sound like I'm bragging?" She shrugged. "Well, I am."

Erin beamed. "Good. I have to tell you, your confidence is really encouraging."

Erika chuckled. "Now is not a time she needs a modest baker."

Ethan let out a rumble of laughter. "Lizzie? Modest about baking? Never. But then, why should she be?"

Lizzie granted him an approving nod. "White cake?" she asked Erin.

Erin said, "We wanted pink champagne cake. And can you add some vanilla mousse filling with the raspberry?"

"You've got it. I'll need to get with your florist. Gerbera daisies in your colors would be nice, trailing in a spiral up over the tiers…"

Erin blinked. "How did you know?"

Lizzie shrugged again. "I can do some pretty white fondant flowers, too, for another accent, as well as edible pearls." She turned her notebook around so that the other two women could see her sketch of the cake.

Erika made a pleased sound.

Erin was beaming. "Oh, it's perfect. Just as I pictured it." She set down her coffee cup. "And I've got my checkbook." She grabbed for the bag she'd hooked on the back of her chair. "I can pay you right now."

Lizzie put up a hand.

But Ethan was the one who spoke. "No way. Consider it your wedding present."

Erin looked stunned. "But I couldn't possibly… No, that's not right. It's too much. I know what a cake like this costs."

Ethan held firm. "You paid once for your cake. Not again."

"Ethan, you're a prince. Really. But it's way too much work for Lizzie. It's not fair to ask her to give her time and talent away like that."

Lizzie spoke up then. "Don't you worry. As I said, I'm honored to create your cake for you. I'm going to *love* baking your cake for you, I promise you."

"And *I* promise," said Ethan, with that melting look that broke all the girls' hearts, "that I'll pick up the tab. It won't cost Lizzie a penny."

Lizzie reached over and put her hand on Erin's slender arm. "Ethan will take care of me. Count on it. He always does."

Before the two women left, Erin invited Lizzie to the rehearsal dinner the next night.

"I would love to, but I think I need to stay focused, if you know what I mean." Actually, she probably could have fit in the dinner, but she wouldn't have been much of a guest because she'd be totally concentrated on all that would need doing the following day. She'd be up at about 4:00 a.m. Saturday, and baking her butt off. Luckily, the wedding was in the late afternoon, giving her a perfectly acceptable window of time to pull it all together.

If she could get all her equipment tomorrow. Which was another reason she didn't want to commit to dinner Friday night. She could still be running around madly then, trying to scare up cake boards or the right size pans.

"The three of us, then," said Erin. "You, me and Erika. We're taking a girls' night out as soon as Corey and I get back from our honeymoon."

Lizzie liked the sound of that. "It's a date."

"I'll call you tomorrow," promised Erika. "In case there's anything you think of that I might be able to help with."

"Thanks. That would be terrific."

And then, in a flurry of goodbyes and thank-yous, Corey's bride and Dillon's wife were gone.

With a sigh, Lizzie sagged against the front door.

Ethan stood in the arch to the living room. "You're amazing." He looked at her with affection and appreciation in those gorgeous dark eyes.

She felt really good, she realized, basking in her boss's admiration—and excited over the cake she would create. "I like them. Both of them. And this is going to be fun."

"What can I do?"

"Stick around for about an hour while I make some calls?"

"You got it."

"Then I'll let you know what I need from you."

Dark eyes gleamed. "See? You already love it here."

She had to confess, "Okay, it's not as bad as I imagined it."

"Not as bad?" His voice coaxed her.

"Ethan, for crying out loud, what do you want from me? We've only been here half a day."

"You love it."

She pushed off the door frame and stood tall on her own two size-ten-and-a-half feet. "It ain't Texas."

"Lizzie." He spoke in that dark, sweet voice he used with his girlfriends. "You love it."

A strange little shiver went through her. She ignored it and blew a loose strand of hair out of her eyes as she gestured down the central hallway, toward his big, well-appointed home office. "Go…check your email or something. I'll call you when I need you."

Lizzie booted up her own computer in her little square of office space off the kitchen and started checking online to see if she could get the equipment she needed overnighted.

No way. Not to Thunder Canyon, Montana.

She spared a wistful thought for the well-stocked shelves in her *maman*'s bakery. But all that was long gone. And even if she'd managed to keep some of her mother's pans and utensils, they would be in Texas now, useless to her anyway.

So she called a couple of restaurant and kitchen supply places in nearby Bozeman. Both were just closing, but they would be open at nine tomorrow morning. And between them, they had what she was going to need.

She made a list—not only of equipment, but of all her ingredients. And then she called Erin's florist and made arrangements to pick up the multicolored daisies Saturday morning. If she was too busy to go, Ethan would do it for her.

He appeared right then, in the doorway to the kitchen, as if she had called for him. "So? Everything under control?"

She hit Save and then Print. "So far, yes." Faintly, in Ethan's office, she heard the printer start up. "Tomorrow, if you can manage it, I need you."

"I'm all yours."

"Great. You can drive me to Bozeman. The supply stores I found open at nine. I want to be there when they unlock the doors. And we can pick up the perishables before we come back, try and get it all in one trip."

"I can get you there and help with carrying groceries and equipment. Also, I'll bring my platinum card."

"Perfect." Then she remembered. "Corey's bachelor party. It's tonight, right?"

He looked puzzled. "Yeah. So?"

"You'll be out till all hours."

"That's the way a bachelor party tends to work."

"So never mind. I can make the trip tomorrow on my own. I'll bring you receipts. Lots of them."

"Uh-uh. I'll get up in time. And I'll take you."

"I'll believe it when I see it."

He was grinning, looking way too handsome, as he took up the challenge. "And you *will* see it. Just wait."

He was sweet to want to help. She did appreciate that. And she always enjoyed his company. But it didn't matter either way. If he wasn't up by the time she had to go, she'd just take off on her own. No big deal. "Want some dinner? I can throw something together within twenty minutes or so."

He shook his head. "The party's at the Hitching Post, a local watering hole. Dillon rented a private room in the back. Dinner included."

"You guys hire a naked girl to pop out of a cake?"

"Lizzie, Lizzie, Lizzie. Give us more credit than that."

"*Two* naked girls?"

He grunted. "You know the old saying. What happens at a bachelor party *stays* at a bachelor party."

She waved a hand at him. "I know, I know. If you told me you'd have to kill me and all that. Better you just keep your secrets. I'm too young to die."

"Plus, I need you alive to make Erin's wedding cake."

"Right. That, too."

"So…the twins and Rose are staying at Thunder Canyon Resort." His brothers Jackson and Jason were fraternal twins. At thirty, their sister, Rose, was the baby of the family. "I thought I'd wander on up there, see how they're doing, maybe have a look around the resort's main clubhouse a little…"

She almost laughed. "And I need to know your every move, why?"

He lifted one hard shoulder in a half shrug. "Well, I mean, if there's anything you need from me. Anything at all…" Now he was giving her that look again. That sweet, melting look, eyes like dark chocolate.

She braced her elbows on her dinky desk and wrinkled her nose at him. "*What* are you up to?"

He smiled, slow and lazy. "Not a thing. I'm just saying you can count on me to help, that you're a lifesaver for poor Erin and I'm here for you, Lizzie."

She made a shooing motion with both hands. "Out. Go. See you tomorrow."

"You sure?"

"I am positive."

"'Night, then." He turned and left her.

She watched him go, thinking what a great butt he had.

Until she caught herself staring and made herself look away.

After that, for several minutes, she just sat there at her

desk, staring blindly into the middle distance, wondering why he seemed to be pulling out all the stops to be charming and attentive to her the past couple of days.

It was kind of annoying, really. They had an easygoing, best-pals relationship. And suddenly, he was messing with the program, falling all over himself to be available to her, coming way too close to flirting with her.

Worse than whatever he was up to, was the way she seemed to be responding to it. Getting all shivery when he sent her a glance. And…staring at his butt?

Okay, yeah. It was a great butt. But still. It wasn't as if that was news or anything.

Really. The last thing she needed was to start crushing on Ethan. That would be beyond stupid.

Lizzie tossed down her pen and stood up. She smoothed her hair and straightened her plain white sleeveless shirt. *Get over yourself, Landry.* Ethan wasn't up to anything beyond being extra nice to her in hope that she might change her mind about resigning.

And she was not crushing on him. Uh-uh. No way. Not in the least.

Chapter Three

At 3:10 a.m. Friday, Ethan clapped his brother Corey on the shoulder. "You're a lucky man," he said.

"Yes, I am," Corey agreed. "I'll walk you out."

Jackson, who was good and toasted at that point, called, "Hey, where you two goin'? Party's jus' gettin' started. 'S'bad enough Dillon crapped out on us early."

The redhead on his lap giggled. "Yeah, you two. Stick aroun'…"

"I'll be back," promised Corey with a rueful grin.

Jason, across the table from his twin, shook a finger. "You guys are gettin' old," he accused.

Neither Corey nor Ethan argued. The lone bartender, left to close up the place when the party was finally over, shook his head and went on polishing the short bar at the other end of the room. He'd stopped serving at two, per Montana law. But that didn't mean the partiers couldn't bring their own and serve themselves.

Ethan waved and left the private back room of the Hitching Post with the groom at his side. They emerged midway along a dim hallway and went right.

Corey pushed the bar on the heavy door beneath the red exit sign and the cool night air came in around them. He waved Ethan out ahead of him and put down the stop on the door to keep it from latching.

They stood in the quiet parking lot under the sodium vapor lights and Corey asked, "You good to drive?"

Ethan nodded. "Not even buzzed. I couldn't afford to get blasted. I'm taking Lizzie to Bozeman bright and early tomorrow to buy supplies for the wedding cake."

Corey grinned. He was a fine-looking man and took after their mother's side of the family, with lighter hair and eyes than Ethan had. "Got news for you, big brother. Tomorrow is already today."

"Did you have to remind me?"

Corey chuckled, but then he grew serious. "I owe you. *And* Lizzie. You've made Erin very happy." His deep voice softened when he said his bride's name. And it struck Ethan strongly: Corey was deeply in love.

First Dillon. Now Corey.

The Traub brothers were dropping like flies lately.

Not that there was anything wrong with settling down. If a man was interested in that kind of thing.

Corey went on, "I told Erin all about the Texas Bluebell Bakery, about those cream cakes and éclairs that could light up your mouth, and about those pies Lizzie's French mama used to bake. Remember those pies? I loved them all. Especially the sweet-potato pie." Corey stuck his hands in the pockets of his jeans and stared up toward the sky, a dreamy look on his face. "When I think of Cécile Landry's sweet-potato pie, it brings it all back, you know? Being a kid again, before Dad died, when life was simple, when a piece of pie could just make your day…"

Ethan did remember Cécile Landry's pies. "I was partial to the strawberry-rhubarb, myself."

"Oh, God," said Corey with a groan. "The strawberry-rhubarb…"

"Lizzie still bakes a rhubarb pie for me now and then. And they're just as good as her mama's, believe me." Lizzie. He scowled. Lizzie, who thought she was leaving him….

Corey lowered his head. He peered at Ethan more closely. "You're lookin' a little grim."

"Lizzie wants to quit." The words were out before he even realized he would say them. And then he went ahead and elaborated, sounding more annoyed than he meant to. "She's got a dream, you know?"

Corey did know. "The bakery—but you were aware of that. You told me two or three years ago, after the two of you became BFFNB, that she wanted to open a bakery again someday."

"Uh…BFFNB?"

"Best Friends Forever, No Benefits," Corey explained with a self-satisfied grin.

"Very funny—and it doesn't matter that I was aware of her big dream. The point is I never really thought she would ever go through with it. What's wrong with working for me, that's what I want to know?"

"Whoa." Corey stepped back. "You're really upset about this."

Ethan felt embarrassed suddenly. Which was ridiculous. He grunted. "Well, yeah. Yeah, I am. We've got a good thing going, me and Lizzie. And have you any idea how much I pay her?"

"What's that have to do with anything?"

"Just answer the damn question."

Corey answered carefully. "I'm sure it's a lot."

"You bet it's a lot. She's got full medical and dental. She's even got points in TOI."

Corey's brows drew together. "But she wants to get back into her family's business."

"Hold on a second here," Ethan grumbled. "You're my brother. You're supposed to be on *my* side."

"I *am* on your side. But Lizzie's always struck me as the type who gets things done, who sees what she wants and makes sure it happens. She wants to open a bakery."

"It's a phase, that's all. She'll get past it."

Corey only looked at him.

"What?" Ethan demanded.

Corey spoke with exasperating gentleness. "I gotta say I've learned a lot about women since I found Erin. Before Erin, I thought I knew it all. But now I'm kind of getting the picture that I didn't know squat."

"And your point is, exactly?"

"Ethan, I'm only saying I don't think you're going to get very far with a capable, take-charge woman like Lizzie by underestimating her."

"What the hell? Who says I'm underestimating her? And who says I want to *get somewhere* with her?"

"Whoa, brother. You are really turned around about this, aren't you?"

"Turned around? I don't know what you're talking about."

Corey gave him another of those long, unreadable looks. "Why do I get the feeling that you're about to put your fist in my face?"

Because I am, Ethan thought. Which was really all out of proportion to the situation, and he knew that. He dialed it back, going for a slow breath as he ordered his body to relax, take it easy. "Sorry. It's late. I've got a lot on my mind and a bad case of jet lag, you know?"

Corey's expression said he wasn't buying Ethan's excuses, but he let it go. "I hear you. Get a little sleep, okay?" He turned for the propped-open door to go back inside.

Ethan felt like a complete jerk bag—meaning worse than a jerk. More like a whole bagful of jerks. "Corey?"

Corey stopped in midstep, sent a glance over his shoulder. "Yeah?"

"I'm glad you found Erin. Congratulations, man."

Corey smiled then. A real smile. "Thanks. I hope you work it out with Lizzie."

What exactly did he mean by that?

Ethan decided he didn't want to know.

Lizzie was up at seven, showered and dressed and ready to face the day by seven-thirty. She headed for the kitchen fully expecting to brew some coffee, grab some toast and be on her way, alone.

But as soon as she opened the door of her room, her nose told her the coffee was already made.

She entered the kitchen to find Ethan sitting at the table in the breakfast nook. He was freshly shaved and wearing boots, jeans and a casual shirt.

"I got the coffee going," he said. He raised his full mug and took a sip. "I was beginning to wonder if you would *ever* get up."

She made a face at him. But actually, she was pleased that he'd made the effort, and that she would have his company for the next few hours. "Want some eggs?"

"Do we have time?"

"Sure. Scrambled?"

"Great."

She went to work on the food. It didn't take long. She

slid his plate in front of him and put the jam in the center of the table. Then she grabbed her own plate and sat down across from him. They ate in silence, fueling up for the morning ahead. He did look a little tired, she thought. There were shadows beneath his eyes.

"How much sleep did you get?" she asked, as she took their empty plates back to the sink.

"Enough."

She sent him a glance. "Listen, I can manage the trip myself if you want to go back to bed."

"I'm taking you."

"But if you—"

He cut her off. "Look, I don't want to go back to bed. I *want* to drive you. Got it?"

"Uh, sure. Got it." She scraped the plates and put them in the dishwasher. "How was the party?"

"It was fine," he said. His tone told her that the subject was closed, just in case she had any idea of trying to get maybe a sentence or two more out of him. So she left it alone.

A few minutes later, they climbed into Ethan's SUV and were on their way.

In Bozeman, they spent about an hour each at the two restaurant supply places. After that, they visited a community co-op grocery, where there was also a deli. They had lunch there before moving on to their final stop, which was Safeway.

They were on the road back to Thunder Canyon at one-thirty. Lizzie was feeling really good about everything by then. Ethan had been sweet and helpful the whole trip. And she had managed to find everything she needed, which was a considerable relief.

At the house, Ethan helped her carry everything inside. When the back of the big SUV was finally empty and the granite counters in the kitchen were piled high with all she'd bought, he asked, "What else can I do?"

"Not a thing," she told him. "You're my favorite boss in the whole world and you have my undying gratitude." She started emptying the bags—groceries first.

He came around the counter toward her. "I love it when you're grateful." He stopped inches away.

She could smell his aftershave, which was subtle and manly and whispered tastefully of money. Already, there was a shadow of dark beard on his sculpted cheeks. She paused with a flat of free-range eggs in her hands. "You know you're directly between me and the fridge, right?"

"Oops." He gave her one of his famous killer half smiles—and stayed where he was.

With a put-upon sigh, she eased around him and carried the eggs to the roomy side-by-side high-end refrigerator. When she shut the door and turned back to him, he hadn't budged. He was still standing there, watching her. A shiver went through her, one way too much like the one she'd felt the day before, when they stood in the foyer together, after Erin and Erika left.

There were bags on every counter. She could so easily have just started on one of them—and steered clear of him. But that seemed downright cowardly somehow. What was the matter with her, anyway? Afraid to approach Ethan? Made no sense at all.

So she marched back around him and started on the next bag, hauling out a jar of cherry juice.

"Lizzie." His big hand closed over her arm—zap. Like a light tap with a live electrical wire.

Seriously. This could not be happening.

She gritted her teeth and faced him. "What?"

"I'm leaving, don't worry." He spoke quietly now, in a low, burned-sugar voice. And he still had hold of her arm.

In fact, he showed no inclination to let go. "I'll get out of your way…"

By a sheer effort of will, she ignored the scary sensations that were zipping through her and muttered drily, "Promises, promises."

"Just one thing…" His eyes were soft as kitten fur. Was he going to kiss her?

No way.

Gently, she eased her arm free of his hold and fell back a step.

There. Much better. She could breathe again. And the disorienting shivery feeling had passed. "Sure. What?"

"Tonight. The rehearsal dinner. I want you to come with me."

She frowned. "But…I already bowed out on that one."

"I know you did." Now he was all eager and boyish and coaxing. "Change your mind. Come with me. Pete and my mom will be there. And my brothers and Rose. And Erin, of course. And Erika. They're all crazy about you. It will be fun. And you can meet my cousins DJ and Dax, and their wives, Allaire and Shandie, and—"

"Ethan."

He blinked. "Yeah?"

"Is there something…going on with you?"

Now he was the one stepping back. At last. "Going on? What are you talking about?"

"Are you, um, putting moves on me or something?"

His mouth dropped open. "What the hell, Lizzie? What makes you think that?" He looked totally stunned at the very idea.

Which wasn't the least bit flattering and also made her feel like a complete idiot for even suggesting such a thing. Heat flooded up her neck. She just knew her whole face was as red as the jar of cherry juice she still clutched in her hand.

She set the juice on the counter and whirled away from him. "Um..." She pressed her eyes shut, hard, willing away her ridiculous blush as well as her own embarrassment at the whole situation. "Sorry. Never mind, okay? Just... forget I asked."

His hands, warm and so strong, closed over her shoulders—and there it was again, that quivery, scary feeling. She wanted to sink right through the floor. He said gently, "Lizzie..."

She asked again, "What is going on with you, Ethan?"

"Nothing. Come with me to the rehearsal dinner."

She shrugged off his hands and made herself face him once more. "Look, I have a lot on my mind and a lot to do, okay?"

"Well, I know. But you won't start on the cake until, like, the middle of the night or something, right? And you've got everything you need now to get the job done. I just thought, you know, why not take a break, come out and see the family?"

He was right, of course. Now the problem of assembling equipment and ingredients had been solved, she could make it to that dinner, no problem.

But she still felt that he was up to something. Even if he wasn't putting moves on her. "You have some kind of plan. That's it, isn't it? You think that if you're relentlessly charming and helpful and drag me with you everywhere you go, I'm going to give in and decide I don't need to open my bakery, after all." She kept her gaze on his handsome face as she spoke. And she saw how he glanced to the side. Yeah, it was only for a second, and then he was meeting her eyes again. But that slight shift away was enough. She knew then that she'd hit the old nail square on the head.

"Hah," she said. "That's it. That is exactly what's going on with you."

"No. Wrong. That's not true at all." His square jaw was set and his eyes flashed with annoyance.

"Don't lie to me, Ethan. I know what you're doing."

"How do you know that? Next you'll be claiming you can read my mind."

"We have an agreement. That's not going to change."

"It might." He smiled then. A slow smile. The smile of a man who never let anything stand in his way when he wanted something, a man used to getting what he wanted in pretty much everything eventually. "You never know."

"Ethan, are you listening?"

"Of course."

"I'll say it slowly. I'm not going to the rehearsal dinner, thank you." She exaggerated each word, just to make sure he understood.

He leaned against the counter and folded his muscular arms over his broad, deep chest. "And that proves…what?"

"I'm not trying to prove anything. I just don't want to go. I want to unpack these groceries and relax, go to bed nice and early. I intend to make Erin's cake spectacular. I consider it a point of professional pride."

"We both know it will be great because you're baking it."

"Thank you."

"Come on." His voice was soft again. "You have to eat dinner…"

"And I will. Here. Quietly. Alone."

"Oh, what? Like it's some kind of…Zen thing?" Now he was razzing her, pure and simple.

She kept her voice level when she answered. "Yes, Ethan. Let's call it a Zen thing—in fact, you can call it whatever you want. What you need to get through your head is that I'm not going with you to that rehearsal dinner."

"What if I said I wanted you there for professional reasons?"

"Well, that would be a flat-out lie. And I would still say no."

Those fine lips of his curled in what could only be called a sneer. "These are supposed to be *my* two months, remember? You're supposed to be doing what *I* want when I want it."

Now she was getting a little bit angry. "Suddenly, I'm your...indentured servant? Is that where you're going with this?"

He made a sound in his throat. An embarrassed kind of sound. Good. He *should* be embarrassed. "Uh. No. No, of course not."

"Well, great. Because being your slave is not going to work for me, Ethan. Even though you're about the best friend I've got in the world, and I want you to be happy, *I* need to be happy, too. I like a challenge and I'm thrilled to go the extra mile and create this cake for your new sister-in-law. But I will not be dragged to that dinner just because it's part of your campaign to make me change my mind about what I want to do with my life. Do you understand?"

He no longer lounged against the counter. He'd drawn himself up straight. And for a moment, he looked as if he might continue the argument. But he caught himself. He raked a hand through that thick almost-black hair and muttered, "Gee, Lizzie. I didn't mean for you to get all het up."

She drew a slow breath and forced a wobbly let's-make-peace smile. "I'll say it once more. I'm not going. And can we be done with this conversation now? Please?"

Something hot and angry flashed in his eyes, his real

feelings breaking the surface—and then vanishing again as fast as she had glimpsed them. "Gotta go," he said dismissively.

And he did leave, just like that. He went around her and strode out through the arch to the hallway. She longed to stop him, to try and settle things for good with him, to somehow put an end to this strange tension and unrest between them.

But at that moment, she didn't see how to settle anything. She told herself that at least she'd held her ground on the issue of the rehearsal dinner, that she'd explained to him—for the umpteenth time—that she *was* moving on and there was nothing he could do about it.

She decided, for now, just to let it be.

The rehearsal at Thunder Canyon Community Church started at four. Afterward, they all headed for the resort and the dinner in the Gallatin Room, which was the resort's best restaurant.

Ethan, as one of the groomsmen, attended both functions. At the dinner, he ended up with his big brother Dillon—the best man—on one side and his mom on the other. Both his brother and his mom asked him if something was bothering him.

He lied and said, "Not a thing," picturing Lizzie's obstinate face in his head, promising himself that one way or another, she was going to see the light within the next eight weeks and realize she loved her job with him and could never leave.

After the dinner, almost everyone wanted to call it a night to be fresh for the big day tomorrow. Not the twins, though. Jackson and Jason were raring to go. They had plans, plans that consisted of continuing the all-night bachelor party from the evening before. They headed down to the Hitching Post to listen to some live music and party some more.

Ethan went with them. Not because he was dying to party so much, but because he wasn't ready to go home. Home was where Lizzie was.

And tonight, that didn't seem all that welcoming a place.

Plus, he figured it wouldn't hurt to keep an eye on his younger brothers. They could get rowdy. Since Dillon had gone home with Erika, and Corey said he needed a good night's sleep because he was getting married the next day, that left Ethan to step up and keep furniture and glassware from getting broken. Not to mention that someone had to be the designated driver.

Jackson, especially, seemed intent on having himself the wildest weekend on record. He'd been blessedly silent for the toasts at the rehearsal dinner. But at the Hitching Post, he raised one full glass after another. He toasted the picture of the almost-naked lady over the bar. And he toasted man's freedom from apron strings and fancy weddings. He flirted shamelessly with every pretty woman in the place.

Ethan also met more than one good-looking woman that night. He flirted, too, a little. Why not?

But he didn't have the heart to ask a pretty girl if she might like to come on home with him. Since Lizzie had been making noises about quitting, he hadn't felt much like hooking up. Sometimes in life, even for a guy who liked women a lot, there were more important things than sex.

When the Hitching Post closed at 2:00 a.m., Ethan managed to coax his two liquored-up brothers into his SUV. They rolled down the windows and sang stupid drinking songs all the way up Thunder Mountain to the resort. It was past three when he finally got them into their rooms and down for the night.

Back at his house, everything was quiet and dark.

Lizzie would be awake within the hour, he knew, to get going on the cake. He considered waiting up for her, maybe brewing her some coffee so it would be ready when she needed it.

Maybe making peace with her...

But in the end, he only shook his head and climbed the stairs to the master suite.

There would be no peace with Lizzie. He knew that. Not while she was so set on leaving him.

Lizzie was up at four, as planned, and got right to work. She didn't see Ethan all morning. Apparently, it had been a long night and he was sleeping in.

Or maybe he was just avoiding her after their argument yesterday.

That was fine. She had a lot to do and no spare time for worrying about smoothing things over with him.

Everything went off without a hitch. She was putting the finishing touches on the decorations at one-thirty that afternoon.

The resort manager, Grant Clifton, was kind enough to send a van and a couple of big, strong guys to Ethan's house to pick up the wedding cake. They arrived at two. With Lizzie supervising, the guys got the cake into the van. One sat in back to protect the cake against any possible mishap during the drive. Lizzie followed them up the mountain to the resort.

She breathed a huge sigh of relief when they got the cake into the ballroom and onto the cake table without serious incident. A few of the gerbera daisies looked wobbly, though. Lizzie was carefully straightening them—each one with its stem in a tiny separate tube of water—when the bride appeared.

Erin Castro let out a cry of sheer joy. "Oh, Lizzie! I swear, it's the most beautiful thing I've ever seen!" She grabbed Lizzie in a hug.

Lizzie laughed and hugged her back. "I'm so glad it's what you wanted."

Erin hugged her harder. "What I wanted? It's more than that. It's…my dream cake."

As resort staff bustled around them, getting the ballroom ready for the reception that evening, Lizzie and Erin stood side by side, their arms around each other's waists, and admired Lizzie's creation. It was really quite something, each graduated tier white and smooth as driven snow, draped in fondant flowers and edible pearls, crowned with the bright-colored daisies.

"Perfect," said Erin.

"Good." Lizzie nodded. "My job here is done."

Erin turned to her again. "You know what? We really need you right here in Thunder Canyon."

"Need me? For what?"

"Corey told me all about your family's bakery in Midland. He said you're planning to open a new bakery there."

"Yes, I am."

"Well, how about opening one here instead?"

Lizzie was flattered. "I'm honestly touched that you think I'd fit in here."

"I don't think it. I *know* it." Erin turned and took both of Lizzie's hands. "I'm only saying, you know, just consider it, give it some thought?"

It wasn't going to happen. But then again, Lizzie was finding she really did like this charming mountain town and the people who lived in it. Why jump straight to an unqualified no? "Sure. I'll think about it."

"Great—and I've got to get moving." Erin grabbed

Lizzie in one last hug. "Hair. Makeup. It never ends. So… six?"

"I'll be there. I can't wait."

Lizzie went back to the house, which she found empty.

Still no sign of crabby Ethan, which was fine. Until she figured out how to smooth things over with him, *and* make him see that he had to get real and accept that she was not giving up on her lifelong dream, well, there wasn't much point in dealing with him anyway.

They would only end up getting into another argument.

She went to work cleaning up the kitchen. And when that was done, she took a long, lazy bath. She put a lot of straightening gel in her hair, blew it dry and took a long time with the flat iron. It turned out great, falling in soft waves to her shoulders, smoother and sleeker than she'd dared to hope. She also lingered over her makeup, getting it just right.

Her dress was a vivid royal blue, sleeveless, with a V-neck and a swingy hemline. She had gorgeous dressy blue sandals with very high heels to go with it and some fabulous chandelier earrings with cobalt-blue stones.

Lizzie was a realist. She was no great beauty and she knew it; her nose was too big, her jaw a bit too strong. Her *maman* had been petite and lovely. Lizzie, though, took after her tall, broad-shouldered dad.

"Stand up straight, ma chère,*"* her *maman* always used to say. *"Be proud. There is no beauty like that of a tall, proud woman."*

Lizzie had always tried to take her mother's advice to heart. Tonight, in five-inch heels, she would tower over a good portion of the men at the reception. So be it.

When she checked herself out in the full-length mirror

on the back of her bathroom door, she felt totally satisfied with what she saw. She twirled in a circle and loved the way the hem of her blue dress swung out around her.

Yeah, she would definitely do. With a last wink at her own image, she hustled into the bedroom to grab her blue satin clutch.

The light tap came at her door just as she was about to open it. Her heart rate accelerated at the sound.

Sheesh. No reason to get all breathless and fluttery just because Ethan had decided to be a gentleman after all and not make her go to his brother's wedding alone.

She pulled the door wide.

And there he was in all his gorgeous, manly splendor. Freshly shaved and showered, looking like a *GQ* cover model in a tux that must have cost a bunch. "Ready?"

She laughed and did a little twirl right there in the doorway and the dress swirled out around her like the petals of a flower. "What do you think?"

"You look terrific." He said it in a grouchy tone, but somehow also managed to sound as if he actually meant it.

"Why, thank you. You're not so bad yourself." She reached for his arm. He surprised her and gave it, tucking her fingers companionably just below the crook of his elbow, over the rich, dark fabric of his jacket.

Yes, she felt that thrill again, the hot little shiver that formed at the point of contact and kind of quivered its way up her bare arm, leaving goose bumps in its wake. But it wasn't so bad, really, now that she was getting used to it.

In fact, if she were honest with herself, she would have to admit that it felt kind of nice.

Wait. Scratch nice. It felt better than nice. It felt pretty wonderful.

* * *

It was the wedding of the year, everyone agreed.

Or at least, of the year so far.

Lizzie thought it was wonderfully romantic.

The handsome old, white clapboard church was decorated with thousands of bright summer flowers and every pew was full. Corey's brothers and stepdad stood up with him. And Erin's bridesmaids looked like summer flowers themselves, each in a different-colored bright satin gown. Erin was a vision in white as she floated down the aisle to meet her groom.

More than one sniffle could be heard from the pews during the exchange of vows. And an audible sigh went up when Corey finally kissed his bride.

The minister announced, "May I present to you Mr. and Mrs. Corey Traub."

Lizzie, in a back pew, heard somebody down the row whisper, "Who's that?" as the bride and groom turned to face their wedding guests.

"I don't know," was the murmured response.

Lizzie glanced over her shoulder to see a tall, lean man silhouetted in the open doors from the vestibule. He wore old jeans, a wrinkled shirt and a black Stetson with the brim dipped low, hiding his face, so that all she could see was a square jaw stubbled with beard.

More people were starting to whisper.

"What in the world…?"

"Never seen him before…"

There were rustling sounds everywhere as the guests turned to see what all the whispering was about.

The mystery man stepped back. He disappeared from the open doorway. And then Dillon Traub, the best man, came striding down the side aisle, slipping out after the stranger.

The organist started playing again and everyone faced front once more as the radiant bride and her handsome groom walked back up the aisle arm in arm.

The reception, in the flower-and-satin-bedecked resort ballroom, was fabulous, Lizzie thought. Dinner was served at eight.

Lizzie, as Ethan's de facto date, was seated with him and the rest of the wedding party at the main table. Everyone made a point to greet her and tell her what a splendid job she'd done on the cake.

Ethan seemed to have put aside his frustration with her, at least for the evening. It was almost like old times, she thought, like back before she'd ever even hinted that she might be moving on. He joked with her and they shared the knowing glances they used to share all the time.

She realized she'd missed their friendship lately, during the pitched battle over her right to define her own future. She'd missed the way they laughed at the same things, the way they could look at each other and know what the other was thinking.

Right after the food was served, she heard Pete Wexler asking Dillon about the mystery man who'd appeared at the back of the church. Dillon said something about a very old and dear friend who was "going through a rough time." Lizzie noticed the speaking glance Dillon shared with his wife. The look on Erika's face said she knew exactly what was going on with guy in the black cowboy hat.

Lizzie waited for Pete to ask more questions.

But then Claudia, on Pete's other side, put her hand over Pete's and whispered in his ear. He turned to his wife. And the subject of the mystery man was forgotten.

Shortly after the exchange between Dillon and Pete,

Ethan leaned close to Lizzie and said for her ears alone, "Help me keep an eye on Jackson, will you?"

"What's up with him anyway?" she asked. Jackson looked as though he'd had way too much to drink, even though the evening was just getting started.

"Basically, he's decided marriage is a crock," Ethan told her. "And he's been wasted pretty much straight through since Thursday night."

"Charming," she muttered, meaning it wasn't. Jackson had always been something of a bad boy, but tonight he had the look of a man about to cause a ruckus. "I'll watch him."

"Thanks." Ethan's voice was velvet soft.

She looked into his deep, dark eyes and thought how a woman could drown staring in those eyes—well, *some* women anyway.

But not Lizzie.

Uh-uh. She loved Ethan dearly, but as a friend and nothing more.

Or so she kept telling herself….

After the meal, before the toasts and the cutting of the cake, there was music. Corey led Erin out onto the floor in front of the long main table for their first dance as man and wife. Lizzie got a little misty-eyed just watching them; they looked so happy together.

As the floor filled with swaying couples, Lizzie visited with Erika, spent some time chatting with Ethan's mom and then with his sister, Rose.

Rose, who worked in PR for TOI in Midland, was radiant in her apple-green strapless satin bridesmaid's gown. She said she loved it in Thunder Canyon and she was coming back the first week of July for a monthlong vacation.

She sipped champagne, her long red hair shining in the light from the crystal chandeliers overhead, and she leaned close and whispered to Lizzie, "I know Ethan is mad that you're leaving, but don't let him get to you. I do wish you luck with your bakery. We all need to follow our dreams." When Lizzie smiled and thanked her, Rose added, "I have a dream myself. A couple of them, actually. I'd like to settle down right here in Thunder Canyon. And find the right guy to settle down *with*."

"Sounds like a great plan to me," Lizzie said.

"Too bad good men are so hard to find. I'm not getting any younger, you know."

Lizzie grinned. "You're barely thirty and you're a knockout. I have faith in you, Rose."

Rose dipped her pretty red head. "Why, thank you, Lizzie."

"But we'll miss you in Midland."

"Midland will just have to get along without me. I love it here." Rose raised her champagne flute in the general direction of a hot-looking guy who stood near the open bar not far from the entrance. She moved in closer to Lizzie and lowered her voice a notch. "See that guy over there? That's Hollis Pritchett, but everyone calls him by his middle name, Cade. Erin suggested I check Cade out—*and* his two brothers."

"Hey," said Lizzie. "Go for it."

"I intend to do just that," Rose replied. Then she stared out toward the dance floor and sighed kind of dreamily. "Aw, isn't that adorable?"

Lizzie followed the direction of Rose's gaze to see a man holding a small bundle in pink, swaying to the music.

"That's Jake Castro, dancing with his daughter," Rose said softly. "Her name is Marlie, I heard. She's just a few weeks old."

"So sweet..."

"Nobody knew Jake had a little girl. Until today. We're all wondering who the mother is…"

Lizzie remembered the mystery man at the back of the church. "Lots of interesting stuff going on around this town."

"Oh, yes, there is," said Rose with a wide grin. "It's another thing I love about the place. Never a dull moment, you know?"

Right then, a male voice shouted, very loud, "Hey, everybody. Everybody, hey!"

The music stopped. Lizzie turned toward the voice. She knew who it was already: Jackson.

He stood, weaving on his feet, in front of the cake table. He had his champagne glass raised high. "Listen up. And listen good. 'Cause I got somethin' important ta say…"

"Uh-oh," muttered Rose.

Lizzie hardly heard her. She was already on the move, working her way through the crowd toward the bad-acting young Traub.

"Marriage?" scoffed Jackson. "I don't like it, not one li'l bit. Marriage is jus' a way to tie a man down. What a man needs, above all, is his freedom!" Jackson blinked. He seemed to be having trouble focusing, which wasn't all that surprising. He had to be completely blasted. "Ladies and genemuns, I give you freedom!"

Right then, Dillon stepped up and muttered something in Jackson's year.

"Quiet?" Jackson blustered. "Uh-uh. No way. You can't silence me. I got a whole lot ta say!"

By then, Dillon had reinforcements. Ethan moved in close and Jason, as well. Even the groom had left his bride and joined the group. Ethan said something and whipped the half-full glass of champagne from Jackson's fist.

That did it.

With a roar of pure fury, Jackson hauled off and punched him. Lizzie let out a cry.

But no one heard her. They were all staring in disbelief as Jackson delivered another blow—that one to Jason, right in the belly.

There was a loud "Oof" from Jackson's twin.

The brawl was on.

Dillon hauled back and busted Jackson in the chops. Ethan got in a good one, too. And Corey grabbed a vase of gerbera daisies from a nearby table and bopped Jackson on the head with it. The vase shattered. Water, glass and daisies rained down.

Jackson didn't even blink. He shook the water out of his eyes, let out a roar of outrage and popped the groom a good one.

Fists flew. For a few seconds, it was hard to tell who was hitting whom.

And then came catastrophe.

Lizzie watched in horror as Jackson, taking a well-placed blow to the chin, flew backward toward the table behind him and the beautiful, defenseless six tiers of pink-champagne, daisy-bedecked wedding cake.

Chapter Four

Claudia Traub shouted, "Boys! Stop this now!"

And poor Erin screamed, "No! Not my cake!"

And then, at the last possible second before the cake met its end, a miracle happened.

Somehow, Ethan managed to slide in between the airborne Jackson and the cake table. He caught his younger brother before he landed, and turned, redirecting the momentum of Jackson's fall so it took them both sideways to the floor.

The table shook a little. A few bright daisies dropped to the linen tablecloth. But the cake, incredibly, remained whole.

Jason, still on his feet, was raring to fight some more. But his older brothers had more sense. Dillon grabbed him by one arm and Corey took the other.

"Easy, Jase. Ease it down now," Dillon soothed.

By then, Lizzie had reached the danger zone.

She dropped to her knees beside the fallen Ethan and his troublemaking younger brother. "Ethan, are you okay?"

Ethan grunted. Jackson was sprawled on top of him. "Get this idiot off me." He gave a shove.

Jackson, with a groan, rolled off of Ethan and onto the floor.

Ethan scrambled to his knees. He wasn't trusting Jackson to not make more mischief. He had a tight grip on his brother's right hand and he pushed Jackson over all the way onto his stomach and shoved his captured fist up between his shoulder blades.

Jackson pounded the floor with his free hand and groaned again. "Hey, cut it out. That hurts, damn it!"

"You going to behave yourself now?"

Jackson muttered a few choice words. "Let me up."

"I'll need your promise that you're through busting up the place."

"Fine. All right. I'm done in."

Suddenly, Claudia was there. "Ethan. Now, now. It's all right. I'll look after him...."

Ethan scowled. "He's an animal, Ma. Watch out."

The fight seemed to go out of Jackson then. He went limp on the floor. "Awright, awright. I'll behave. I swear I will."

Ethan let go of him. "What a damn fool," he muttered as he stood. Shaking his head, he reached down a hand to Lizzie, who still crouched on the floor.

She took it and he pulled her up. As she rose and stood beside him, she had the craziest urge to throw her arms around him and kiss him silly.

But somehow, she kept her head. She said, "My hero! You saved the cake."

He threw back his dark head and laughed, drawing her closer, draping a big arm across her shoulders. Around them, more than one guest was laughing, too. There was even a smattering of applause.

Someone told the small band to start playing again. And everyone went back to dancing and visiting and whatever else they'd been doing before the fight broke out.

Claudia, grim-faced, helped Jackson to his feet. "Are you hurt, son?"

Jackson worked his jaw, pressed a hand to his ribs. "It only hurts when I laugh. Or breathe. Or talk."

"So shut up," Corey suggested. "At this point I wouldn't mind if you stopped breathing, too."

"Corey," said Claudia reproachfully. "It's enough."

By then, Corey and Dillon had let go of Jason, who had backed away a little and was hanging his head. Erin had run to her new husband. Erika stood with Dillon, her hand in his.

A guy in a resort uniform was cleaning up the broken glass from the shattered vase.

Pete stepped up and put an arm around his wife. "Well, boys, I have to say it. Looks like the Texas Traubs have officially arrived in Thunder Canyon. This town will never be the same."

The party lasted until late into the night.

It was after two when Ethan took Lizzie home.

He pulled the big, black SUV into the garage and turned off the engine as the door rumbled down behind them. Then he draped an arm on the steering and turned to her. "It was fun." His white teeth flashed with his smile.

"It certainly was."

"How about some coffee?"

She felt good right then, about everything. He'd been so easy to be with all evening, not a single dark look or snide remark. She as if like she had her best friend back at last. "Sure."

They went into the kitchen and she brewed the decaf. "Want a cookie?" She sent him a glance where he sat at the table. "I've got some white-chocolate chip and oatmeal-raisin, too."

He shook his head. "Don't tempt me. Two pieces of wedding cake's my limit for one night."

She turned and leaned against the counter as she waited for the coffee to drip. "Is Jackson...all right?"

He arched a dark eyebrow. "Other than being a total wild-ass crazy man, you mean?"

"I'm serious. I've never seen him quite so rowdy as he was tonight. I mean, he was pretty wasted. And starting a brawl at a wedding isn't exactly what I'd call rational behavior."

"He's fine," Ethan reassured her. "Going through a few changes maybe. But he's tough. He'll work out whatever's bothering him, you watch."

She gave a weary shrug. "If you say so..."

"Hey." Ethan got up from his chair and came to her. He'd taken off his bow tie some time before and his snowy tux shirt was open at the neck. He looked totally relaxed and a little bit tired, and she found herself thinking what a great guy he was. A wonderful friend. The best boss ever. "Don't worry about Jackson." He stopped just inches from her.

And it was...a little overwhelming somehow—his standing so close that she could feel the heat of his body, with her backed against the counter.

Why should his being close bother her now? She'd danced with him at the reception. He'd put a companionable arm around her more than once during the evening, and it had all seemed so easy and friendly.

But now, alarms were going off inside her head. Maybe it was that it was just the two of them, alone in the quiet kitchen in the middle of the night.

Suddenly, his being close to her felt scarily intimate rather than fun and companionable. She hadn't even realized she'd tipped her head down to avoid staring into his eyes—until he touched her chin with a brush of his warm hand.

"Lizzie…" He whispered her name so tenderly, just the way a lover might. Reluctantly, she lifted her head. His eyes were waiting, dark and soft and tempting. A smile quirked one corner of his mouth. "Okay?"

She frowned. "About?"

"Jackson?" he prompted, his eyes lighting with amusement that she had already forgotten her concern for his wild younger brother.

She felt her cheeks coloring. Did he notice? "Uh, Jackson. Right."

"Don't worry about him."

"Well, okay. I won't."

His smile widened. "Good."

Behind her, the coffeemaker sputtered. "Coffee's ready," she said too brightly, bringing up her hands between them and pushing lightly at his chest. "And you're crowding me."

He seemed amused. "Can't have that." And he turned and went back to his chair.

The moment—scary, unreal and way too intimate—had passed. Lizzie suppressed her sigh of relief and turned to get down the coffee cups.

Lizzie in a blue dress.

Ethan thought she looked really good in that dress. Tall and strong and curvy. And so…capable.

How had it happened that he was starting to find "capable" downright sexy?

Strange. He'd always gone for more decorative women. Gorgeous, petite blondes with wide eyes and pouty lips, the kind of women who required constant pampering. High-maintenance women. Women nothing at all like Lizzie.

He would bring them home and Lizzie would cook them wonderful meals—meals they hardly touched to remain a size zero. The women he dated always liked Lizzie because she treated them gently. Kindly. With affection and real care. They always mentioned that she pampered them.

Ethan sat back in the kitchen chair. He watched her get down the cups and pour them each some coffee.

Friday afternoon, when he'd gotten so pissed at her for not going with him to the rehearsal dinner, she'd asked him if he was putting moves on her.

That she would even imagine he would do such a thing had shocked him at the time. After all, Lizzie meant the world to him in a number of ways.

But not in *that* way.

Or so he'd always thought. Until tonight.

Maybe it was the fear of losing her that had him starting to see her in a different light. Seeing her as a woman—a woman who was attractive to him.

Not that he would ever actually do anything about this new awareness he had of her. Not that he would hit on her or anything. That would be beyond stupid. He really liked women, but he'd never gotten anything going with someone he worked with.

And he never would. It was not only a matter of principle, but it was also about common sense. Love affairs ended. Feelings got hurt. It became too uncomfortable, being around each other all the time. It got in the way of the job.

And then either she would quit, or he would have to ask her to leave.

He'd end up with exactly the result he was supposed to be knocking himself out to prevent: losing Lizzie.

Uh-uh. The point was to get her to see that working for him was something she wanted to keep doing.

But it sure was fun flirting with her, keeping her a little off balance, keeping her wondering what exactly he was up to.

She set his cup in front of him, carried hers to the chair across the table and sat down. She sipped, glancing up as she swallowed—catching him watching her. "What?" she demanded, a slight frown puckering the smooth skin between her brows.

He picked up his coffee. "Not a thing."

"I have an idea," Lizzie said at noon the next day, Sunday, when he came down for breakfast. She poured his coffee and set it in front of him.

"I just got up," he grumbled.

"I realize that." She stood at his side, already dressed in jeans and a short-sleeved red shirt. The kitchen smelled of wonderful things. Muffins. Bacon. In fact, it had always seemed to him that *she* smelled of wonderful things. Any number of wonderful things—vanilla, chocolate, fresh strawberries, toasted pecans. Whatever she happened to be baking at the time.

"So where are the muffins?" he asked. "And can I have some bacon, please?"

"I've been thinking," she said, gazing down at him.

He grunted. "It's too early for thinking. Breakfast?"

"Just listen for a minute. Please?"

"Fifty-nine seconds, fifty-eight…"

She grabbed his shoulder, gave it a hard squeeze. "Say you're listening."

"Ouch. Stop. Okay, what?"

She let go. Strangely, he found himself almost wishing she hadn't. And she asked, "You're not going back to Midland, are you? This isn't a temporary thing, your being here. You're going to make the oil-shale thing work."

"No, no and yes. Breakfast? Please?"

She went to the counter, got the plateful of golden muffins, carried them back to the table and set them down. "Have a muffin." She went over and took the chair opposite him.

He grabbed a muffin and broke it in half. Still warm. He sucked in the fragrant steam that rose from the sweet, hot center. "Butter?"

She slid the butter dish closer to him.

He buttered the muffin, slanting her a put-upon glance, which she completely ignored.

She folded her hands on the tabletop. "So I was thinking that in spite of what we agreed on in Midland, you are really going to need someone when I go, at least at the office. In fact, maybe *two* someones. An assistant on the job *and* a housekeeper."

Because his plan was that she was going nowhere, he certainly didn't need to worry about who would replace her. But he couldn't say that to her as he had already agreed to let her go at the end of July. So he only grumbled, "What we agreed on is fine. I told you I would hire my own assistant. Now, about that food…"

Her hair was kind of wild around her face, the way it usually was at home. Lizzie had badly behaved hair. At the office, she tried to tame it, but it would always escape and get in her eyes or curl along the sides of her cheeks. Ethan found her hair totally charming.

Right now, though, her mouth had formed a grim line. The grim line wasn't very attractive. When she set her mouth like that, it usually meant she was about to lecture him.

Which was exactly what she proceeded to do. "You have to be realistic. You don't want to be without help work-wise *or* here at home. You're not going to like having to waste your time finding the people that I can easily find for you."

He knew exactly what she was doing. She'd realized she would feel way too guilty just leaving him high and dry with no one to step in and take her place.

What she refused to see was that he *wanted* her guilty, that he was completely shameless when it came to keeping her. If guilt would do it, guilt it would be. At least until she came to her senses and realized that staying with him was actually what she really wanted after all.

He said, "We've been through this. We have an agreement. Just stick to your end of it and I'll stick to mine."

"But Ethan—"

"How about over easy?" He sniffed the air. "And is that home fries I smell?"

She made a low, growling sound and blew a loose strand of hair out of her eyes. "You are so obstinate."

"Lizzie, I'm starving here."

Her chair scraped the floor as she jumped up and hustled over to the stove. He reached for a second muffin.

Three minutes later, she set a plate of eggs, potatoes and beautiful, crisp bacon in front of him. "There. Shut up and eat."

He caught her hand before she could escape his side and said in the warm, low voice he usually reserved for the women he dated, "Lizzie, come on…"

She glared down at him. Her mouth had gone from grim all the way to mutinous. "I *am* leaving, Ethan. You might as well let me make sure you have what you need when I go." Her hand felt good in his. Strong. Not small, but still with a certain womanly softness. He thought how simple it would be to pull her down onto his lap. To silence her by covering her mouth with his.

But of course, he wasn't going to do that. It was one thing to be willing to play on her guilt, but it was another to get something started that could only end in a bad outcome for both of them. "What if what I need is you?"

She sucked in a sharp breath through her mouth, which was suddenly soft enough for kissing. He thought how good she looked, with her hair misbehaving and her lips slightly parted. But the kissable expression lasted for maybe only a second. Then she was scowling. "Let go of my hand, please." He did. She jerked it around behind her back, as if she feared he might grab for it again. And then she whirled and went to the counter, where she took her sweet time filling another cup with coffee. Finally, she turned, leaned against the counter and sipped. "You let me know if you change your mind about letting me find the right people for you."

"Will do." He got busy on breakfast.

She sipped some more, watching him eat. "I need to get to the store today. And then I thought I'd finish pulling the house together. I got kind of behind the curve when I took on Erin's wedding cake."

He wanted to ask how she could even consider leaving him. They were a great team and he was going to do big things. It was only going to get better from here on out—for both of them.

But all he said was, "Whatever you think. Try and get a little time just for yourself. Tomorrow, I'll need you up at the resort all day."

* * *

The next morning, Lizzie took her own vehicle up to the resort. That way, at the end of the day, if Ethan decided he wanted to hang around and do a little socializing, she would be free to take off.

Lizzie was there at 9:00 a.m. in the resort office when Ethan met with Grant Clifton, the general manager. Connor McFarlane, the resort's most recent major investor, was there, as well. Connor was heir to the exclusive McFarlane House hotel chain.

Grant, tall and lean with dark blond hair, was a local rancher-turned-businessman. Connor, who had dark hair and eyes and a brooding intensity about him, had recently married a local woman, a schoolteacher named Tori Jones. Tori, it turned out, was close friends with Allaire Traub, the wife of Ethan's cousin DJ.

Dillon stopped in at about nine-fifteen, just to make sure that Ethan didn't need him or have any questions for him. Lizzie knew that Dillon wasn't the only Texas Traub pushing for TOI to put money into the resort. Corey was, too. And he would no doubt have dropped by with Dillon—if he hadn't been off on his honeymoon.

They met in a conference room, the four men and Lizzie. For a while there was the usual getting-to-know-you chitchat about Thunder Canyon, about how Lizzie and Ethan were settling in at the house Ethan had leased, about family and friends. Lizzie played hostess, getting everyone coffee, passing the pastry around.

After an hour or so of visiting, Dillon left them. "Call me if you need me…"

Ethan promised he would.

They got down to business, poring over the extensive documentation Grant had provided, discussing revenues and expenses, income versus outlay. Lizzie had her laptop.

She took detailed notes as the men worked, simultaneously keeping track of any messages or calls from Midland. For now, Ethan had to be available should Roger Jamison need his advice or guidance.

At lunchtime, they all went up to the clubhouse. They ate in the Gallatin Room and then Connor said he had to go.

He turned to Lizzie. "Great to meet you. You're already a heroine here in Thunder Canyon, whipping up that first-class wedding cake for Erin, saving the day at a moment's notice."

Lizzie laughed. "Hardly a heroine. I'm a baker, born and bred. I baked a cake. It's what I do."

"Well, my wife, Tori, said to be sure and tell you that if Ethan will give you an hour or two tomorrow, you should drop by the Tottering Teapot around noon. They serve lunch there—it's all extremely healthy and organic. Homegrown produce. Everything natural, nothing with hormones or preservatives. And they offer about a thousand different varieties of tea. The women in town love it."

"I'll bet," said Ethan in a tone that made it clear you wouldn't be catching him at the Tottering Teapot anytime soon.

Connor chuckled at Ethan's muttered remark and then added, "Allaire Traub will be there, too. And probably several other friends of theirs from town. They would love to have you join them."

It sounded kind of fun actually. "I'll see if I can sneak away tomorrow."

"It's easy to find," Connor said. "On Main near Pine Street, in what we call Old Town."

"We have Old Town and New Town," Grant explained. "Old Town is the original town, built when the first settlers came here. It's just east of Thunder Canyon Road. New Town is bigger. It's farther east, where they started building, adding on as the town grew."

Connor turned to Ethan. "I'm leaving tomorrow for several days of meetings at McFarlane House headquarters in Philadelphia. Didn't you mention you were going to be traveling, too?"

Ethan nodded. "To Helena at the end of this week and Great Falls next week." Lizzie kept track of his schedule. He would be working on oil-shale acquisition with those trips, negotiating the purchase of mineral rights to some large tracts of oil-rich shale lands.

And she would be with him, laptop and PDA at the ready, taking notes, making his life run as smoothly and efficiently as possible so that he could wheel and deal without getting bogged down in the details.

"When we're both back in town we should all make a day of it," Connor suggested, with a nod at Grant. "Let us show you the property."

Grant chimed in, "We can tour the golf course first, by golf cart. But for most of the property, horseback is the best way to go. You'll really get a feel for the land on the mountain. It's big. And it's beautiful. You do ride?"

"Yes, I do." Ethan had always loved to ride. He offered a hand to Connor and they shook. "A tour on horseback sounds good to me."

Connor left, after which Grant took Ethan around the clubhouse, all five stories and various wings. Lizzie followed along, taking notes.

There were several restaurants on-site, including the Grubstake for casual dining and also DJ's Rib Shack, which was owned and run by Ethan's cousin, the one and only DJ Traub. DJ owned the Rib Shack franchise, with rib restaurants all across the western United States. He was very successful. And he always joked that it was all because of his special secret sauce.

Beyond the Grubstake and DJ's and the Gallatin Room for fine dining, there was also the Lounge, which had a very masculine feel, all dark wood and leather booths and wing chairs. To Lizzie, the Lounge seemed like the kind of place where cattle barons should hang out, drinking whiskey, smoking fifty-dollar cigars and discussing range rights and the fluctuating price of beef on the hoof.

The spa, called the AspenGlow, was decorated in cool greens and soothing grays. It offered every variety of massage under the sun, along with facials and mud wraps and the usual hair, makeup and mani-pedis.

There was even a fully equipped infirmary, so that any guest who got sick or injured could receive immediate care. Dillon, who now ran a clinic in town, had filled in for the resort's regular doctor last year when he'd first moved to Thunder Canyon.

After the tour of the clubhouse, they got a quick look at the stables. The resort kept a number of horses for the use of the guests. Riding lessons were also available.

It was a few minutes before five and they were back at the clubhouse when Grant offered a drink in the Lounge before they called it a day. Ethan said he'd love a drink.

Lizzie took that as her cue to leave her boss and Grant alone for a little quality schmoozing time. "Well, all right, then. If you don't need me, I'll just—"

"Lizzie." Ethan reached out and hooked an arm across her shoulders, pulling her close against his side. "Come on, stick around. Have a drink."

Maybe she shouldn't have been shocked, but she was. Never in all the years she'd worked for him had he put his arm around her during working hours.

Yeah, okay. They were close friends. He'd put his arm

around her several times the night before last, at Erin and Corey's wedding reception. But not at the office, not when she was wearing her admin-assistant hat.

It just wasn't done.

He was watching her face, smiling at her, a smile that teased and challenged. He knew exactly what he was doing.

She wanted to elbow him a good one, right in the ribs. At the same time, she became intimately aware of the hardness of his body, pressed right up against hers. She not only ached to poke him in the ribs, but she also longed to turn in his arms, sighing, to slide her hands up the warm contours of his big chest and link them around his strong neck. To offer her mouth for his kiss.

But she didn't. Lizzie Landry was made of sterner stuff. She didn't jab him in the side and she didn't kiss him, either.

She held it together. "Sorry, I really can't." She ducked out from under his hold. And she sent Grant a grin, just to show the other man that she was in control and not the least fazed by the sudden too-friendly behavior of her boss. "I'm his housekeeper, too," she explained. "*And* his cook." Then she looked straight at Ethan again. He still wore that annoying, overbearing smile. "And I really need to start thinking about what to put together for dinner…"

"No problem," said Ethan. "We'll have a drink with Grant. And then I'll take you out."

Chapter Five

"This is not acceptable," Lizzie said under her breath as the host pulled out a chair for her in the Gallatin Room.

It was just Lizzie and Ethan by then. They'd had that drink with Grant and then Ethan had decided they might as well stay at the resort for dinner.

"Lizzie, Lizzie, Lizzie," Ethan chided from across the way-too-intimate corner table for two. "Come on, have a scat."

Reluctantly, she took the chair and thanked the host, who then handed her a lushly tooled leather menu that was practically as big as their table.

"Your waiter will be right with you," he said.

Ethan thanked him and he went away.

She lowered her giant menu and leaned toward the too-good-looking, totally annoying man across the table. "You keep saying you're not up to anything," she accused softly, in an effort not to broadcast her issues with him to the whole graciously appointed restaurant with its fabulous view of snowcapped Thunder Mountain. "And then you act like you're up to something."

He looked at her with reproach in those dark chocolate eyes. "I'm taking you out for a nice dinner after a long day of hard work. I'm only being an appreciative boss. Why would you think that I'm up to something?"

"Because you—"

He stopped her with a raised hand and sent a glance in the direction of the guy in the snowy-white shirt, black trousers and black vest who was approaching their table. "Our waiter's here."

Ethan ordered a very pricey bottle of Cabernet. The waiter left them. "Now, you were saying?"

"You know," she said pleasantly, "I think I'll wait to ream you a new one until we have the wine and our food."

He gave her that slow killer smile of his. "An excellent idea."

The waiter returned with the wine. Ethan tasted it, gave a nod of approval and the waiter poured. They both ordered filets and baked potatoes, with house salads to start.

Again, the waiter departed.

Ethan raised his wineglass. "To success in Thunder Canyon."

"I'm suspicious of just about everything you do lately." She lifted her glass, too. "But I see no reason not to drink to that."

"Lizzie." He pretended to look hurt. "Be nice."

"I *am* nice. Until you push me too far." She clinked her glass with his and sipped. It was delicious, smooth and layered. "Really good," she told him grudgingly as she set her glass back down.

He beamed in pride, as if he'd stomped the grapes himself. "I thought you would like it." He sat back in the chair and studied her for a moment. She wondered what over-the-line move he was going to make next. But then he only asked the sort of question he often asked her when he was in the middle of deciding on an investment or an acquisition. "So, what do you think of the resort? Just your impressions after today."

She glanced around the dining room. There was no one nearby to overhear her remarks. And she kept her voice low. "I think it's a beautiful facility and I think Grant runs a very tight ship. From what I saw of the books, they're doing better than they were a year ago. I think it's impressive, the range and quality of services...."

He was leaning closer. "But?"

"It's so ambitious. Not only the clubhouse and the endless array of high-end options, the shops, the spa, the three restaurants, the Lounge *and* the coffee bar. I noticed there are also condos up the mountain, and private cabins, too."

"Yeah. And?"

"And it's way out here in the middle of..." she hesitated. She really liked Thunder Canyon. Four days since they'd arrived from Midland. And already it seemed disloyal to say anything critical about the charming little town.

He prompted, "In the middle of nowhere. Right?"

She gave a low laugh. "That sounds a little harsh, doesn't it?"

"I wouldn't call Thunder Canyon nowhere exactly. Tourists love towns like this."

"True," she said, meaning it. "It's the kind of place most people think doesn't exist anymore. The classic, homey, welcoming small town."

"And this is a destination resort," he reminded her. "That's supposed to be part of the draw, that you travel to get here, and that makes it more...exclusive. But I know what you mean. It's not that *easy* to get here. And with the economy still not exactly booming, well, luxury destinations are going to continue to take a hit."

She could always read him. "Still, you want to invest."

He took another slow sip of wine. "Am I that transparent?"

She shook her head. "Only to me. It's the price you pay for having someone who works side by side with you *and* lives in your house." It seemed a good moment to add, "Which is a good reason you might want to split the job again when I go, hire a housekeeper *and* an assistant. Get a little distance from the help. You don't need your employees knowing all your secrets."

His expression had changed, become blank. Unreadable. "I never minded your knowing my secrets. I trust you, Lizzie. Absolutely."

Tenderness welled in her. The thing was, she believed him. She knew very well that he trusted her. As she trusted him. Maybe not so unconditionally as she once had. Lately, her trust was a tiny bit shaky, because he'd refused to acknowledge her need to make her own way now, because he seemed to be putting the moves on her—and yet constantly denied he was doing that.

The waiter came with their salads.

The food provided an excuse not to say anything more for a few minutes, to let those dangerous tender feelings subside.

"Good, huh?" he asked.

"Excellent."

They ate in silence.

She tried to remember how pissed off she was at him. But it was difficult, when he talked about trusting her and she knew that he meant it. When she couldn't help thinking how generous and kind he was at heart, of the ways he'd been there for her when she'd desperately needed a helping hand.

Once, in the first few months that she worked for him, long before she started taking care of his house, when she was simply his assistant at the office and nothing more, her dad had been arrested for drunk driving. Ethan caught her crying at her desk and demanded to know what the problem was. She lied and said it was nothing.

He signaled her into his private office, shut the door, handed her a box of tissues and waited until she gave in and it all came pouring out. She confessed everything. That her dad had never been right after her mom died, that his heart was broken and he didn't know how to heal it. That he'd lost the family bakery while she was away at college and she'd never had any idea what was happening until it was all gone and they were broke. How her father had a drinking problem now and he'd just gotten a DUI. How they'd hauled him off to jail and she didn't have the money to bail him out.

Ethan told her not to worry. That he would take care of it.

And he did. He made calls and got her dad a good lawyer. He paid for everything, made sure that Vernon Landry got community service and counseling rather than jail time. And when Lizzie insisted on paying him back, he told her she was a great worker and deserved a giant bonus exactly equal to the amount he had spent on getting her poor dad out of trouble. She signed that bonus back over to him and he said they were even.

Then, a year and a half ago, when her dad died of a stroke in his sleep, Ethan had been there, offering his broad shoulder to cry on. After the funeral, he'd given her three extra weeks off with pay and a vacation package to Hawaii.

Her injured heart had started to heal there, on the wide sandy beaches under the palms.

Ironically, it was her dad's death that had made it possible for her to start planning on opening her bakery sooner than she'd ever thought could be possible. It had turned out that no matter how broke Vernon Landry had gotten, he'd always made the payments on his life-insurance policy. And Lizzie was his only beneficiary. Between the insurance payout and the great money Ethan had always paid her, she had what she needed now to make her dream come true.

The waiter cleared off their empty salad plates and brought the main course.

"You're way too quiet," Ethan said gently when they were alone again.

She swallowed a bite of tender filet, put on a smile. "Just…thinking."

His eyes were so dark, so deep and soft. "About?"

"The past."

"What about it?"

"Never mind."

"Lizzie…"

She gave him a long, solemn look. "You know exactly what you did, Ethan. You put your arm around me during working hours."

"Lizzie…"

"Don't *Lizzie* me. We have rules between us. Unspoken rules, but rules nonetheless. We never get chummy during working hours. But suddenly, you're throwing an arm around me in front of Grant Clifton, acting like I'm one of your girlfriends or something."

He didn't say anything. He only put down his fork, sat back in his chair and…watched her, a strange, unreadable expression on his face.

Although a hot flush flowed up over her cheeks, she made herself go on. "The other day, I asked you if you were putting a move on me. You denied it. You got all hurt and shocked-looking that I would even suggest such a thing. But still, since we've been here, in Thunder Canyon, you *have* been acting…differently toward me. You know you have."

He sat forward then, picked up his fork again, ate some potato. And then he took his knife and cut another bite of tender steak.

"Will you please just…say something?" She kept her voice low, but there was tension in it that she couldn't hide.

He took his time chewing and swallowing. Finally, he said with no inflection, "I apologize for crossing the line at work. I won't do that again."

"Great," she said tightly. And then she waited for him to continue.

He didn't. "More wine?" He refilled her wineglass even though she hadn't said yes.

The beautiful meal waited in front of her, almost untouched. She picked up her fork and started eating again, her gaze on her plate because the last place she wanted to be looking right then was at the man across from her.

She felt so strange—edgy and angry. With Ethan, with the whole situation between them lately.

Was she being unreasonable, to want more from him in this exchange? He'd dealt with her issue, after all. He'd promised to keep his hands to himself during working hours, which was all she'd been going for when she started this uncomfortable conversation.

But no. Unreasonable of her or not, she was far from satisfied. He'd said nothing about his behavior the rest of the time lately, and his behavior had become seriously suspect. He darn well had to know that.

"Lizzie, come on, don't be mad at me," he finally said softly. Warmly. Gently.

She made herself lift her chin and face him. His dark eyes were waiting. He looked hopeful and worried. Was that how he actually felt? Lately, it was so hard to know with him. "I'm just…confused, that's all."

"Don't be. Everything will be fine. You'll see."

"Fine. What do you mean by fine?"

"I mean, it's all going to work out and there's no need to make a big deal out of nothing."

"Nothing. That's what's going on with you? Nothing?"

He picked up his wine but set it down without drinking any. "Look, it's just a crazy time, that's all. Everything's… changing. Maybe I'm a little on edge, okay? I'm sorry if it seems to you that I'm taking my problems out on you."

She set down her fork. It clinked against her plate. "That is not what I said—or at least, it's not what I meant. I was talking about the way you're always getting close to me. I mean physically close. I was talking about the way you're always…flirting with me lately. The way you've been treating me like I'm one of your pretty little girlfriends when you know very well I'm not."

The hooded look was there in his eyes again. He lounged back in the chair, one muscular arm outstretched, his big hand resting on the snowy linen tablecloth. "Beyond working together, beyond what a great job you do keeping my house for me, we *are* friends, Lizzie. Good friends. We're…BFFNB."

"Uh. Excuse me?"

He gave a lazy shrug. "Best Friends Forever, No Benefits."

She blinked. "Where did you get *that*?"

"It doesn't matter where I got it. It's the truth, right?"

She shook her head. "How do you do that?"

"What?"

"Put me on the defensive when all I asked is why you're suddenly treating me like one of your girlfriends?"

Now he wore a look of endless patience. "I'm only saying that you never minded before if I was affectionate. I'm only saying, yeah. You're right. I shouldn't have put my arm around you while we were working—though if you think back, we were done working at the time, and talking about having a drink in the Lounge."

No wonder his girlfriends never lasted. He probably exhausted them by staying miles ahead of them in any argument. "You know, you could probably convince a stabbing victim that she shouldn't have gotten in the way of the knife."

"Lizzie." He gave her the melting-chocolate look from those amazing dark eyes. "What are you saying? You feel like a stabbing victim?"

"Of course not. I feel like my brain is going to explode before I ever get you to understand what's bothering me."

"But I do understand what's bothering you."

News to her. "Uh. You do?"

"Yeah. You think I'm flirting with you and you want me to stop. You don't like me flirting with you. You find it offensive."

"Wait a minute. So you admit you've been flirting with me?"

"And you find my flirting offensive."

"I didn't say that."

"So...you *do* like it when I flirt with you?"

Lizzie glared at him. And then she picked up her knife and fork for the third time. "Let's just eat. Let's just...move on. Okay?"

He tipped his head to the side and smiled in a wry way. "Sounds like a great idea to me."

* * *

The next morning at breakfast, Lizzie told Ethan she'd like to have lunch with Tori McFarlane and Allaire Traub at that tea shop Connor had mentioned the day before. "I'd like from about eleven-thirty to one-thirty for lunch. Is that too long?"

"Go," he said. "Have a great time."

"Thank you." She set down her coffee cup and gave him a warm smile.

He arched a brow. "Are you flirting with me?"

"Huh?"

"Well, Lizzie, I'm just trying to get clear on what constitutes flirting. Does a smile constitute flirting?"

"Uh, why are we suddenly talking about flirting?"

"Because I need to know. If you smile at me, are you flirting with me?"

"Well, Ethan, no. A smile is not necessarily a sign that someone's flirting with you—and I'm certainly not. You know I'm not."

"So how do you know if *I'm* flirting with *you?* Or if I'm not?"

She had the distinct feeling she was being cornered. And she had no idea how to keep it from happening. "I just…I know. That's all. I just know."

"So you *know* I've been flirting with you."

She scrunched up her nose at him. "I thought we settled this last night."

"Well, I'm just saying that you might think I'm flirting when I'm really not. Maybe I'm just being affectionate. Or friendly. Or maybe I just like you and so I smile at you—like you just did to me."

"Ethan."

"Yeah?" He slathered jam on his sourdough toast.

"It's one thing if you refuse to really talk to me about

any given subject. It's another thing if you refuse to talk to me—and then bring the subject up again when I've already given up on it."

He frowned. "I have no idea what you're saying."

"You know what? At this point, neither do I."

"But if I kissed you, now *that* would definitely be flirting, right?"

"What are you getting at?"

"I've been thinking it over, that's all."

"Thinking *what* over?"

"Kissing you—and don't worry, it won't happen during working hours."

"Ethan!" She gaped. She couldn't help it.

He laughed, a low, deep rumble. "Don't look so shocked."

She knew her cheeks were hot-pink. She sputtered, "Well, it's just…that's not who we are."

"You know, I've been thinking about that, too. About who we are. About how really stupid it is to ruin a good thing—which we definitely would—with flirting and kisses." He paused. "With sex."

She felt breathless. "Well. Then, good. We won't, then. We won't, um, ruin a good thing." She could not sit still suddenly. She grabbed her unfinished plate, jumped up and carried it over to the sink.

Behind her, she could hear him. He had pushed back his chair.

He came toward her much too quietly.

She set her plate on the counter. And after that, she had no idea what to do next. Pretend he wasn't standing right behind her? Whirl and demand that he back off?

But that was the problem. She wasn't sure she really wanted him to back off.

The past few days, when it came to him, she wasn't sure of anything.

"Um. Ethan?" She spoke to the window over the sink that looked out on the side yard.

He touched her. He put his hands on her shoulders, clasping. And it felt so good. "You're trembling…"

Why deny it? "Only a little."

"Come on, Lizzie, turn around." He tugged on her shoulders, urging her to do as he asked.

And she did. She turned to face him. And she was way too aware of the warmth of him, the just-showered scent of him. His eyes found hers. Caught.

Held.

He clasped her shoulders again. "Everything's changing."

"Yes."

"I've been lying to you, Lizzie, saying I accept that you're leaving. I don't accept it. I don't want you to go."

"I know." Tears filled her eyes. Of all things. One got loose and dribbled down her cheek.

He said her name, so softly. With such beautiful tenderness. "Lizzie." And then, "Don't cry." He touched her face with his thumb. He wiped that tear away.

"I'm not," she lied.

And that was when he pulled her closer.

That was when his warm, firm mouth closed over hers for the very first time.

Chapter Six

Kissing Lizzie.

Ethan couldn't believe it. But it *was* happening.

And it felt so good.

He gathered her into him and he deepened the kiss. Enough to taste coffee and strawberry jam, to breathe in the warm, clean heat of her breath. She was…just Lizzie. Special and important and different from any woman he'd ever known. Firm and strong and tall in his arms. Substantial. And yet, soft, too.

Womanly in all the ways he had known she would be.

He framed her obstinate face with his hands, his fingers at her temples, brushed by her wildly curling, ill-behaved hair. Had he known her hair would be so soft? "Lizzie…"

And he kissed her some more.

She made a low, sweet noise in her throat, and she kissed him right back. Eagerly, with the same sweet, passionate enthusiasm she gave to everything—from baking a six-tier wedding cake for his brother's wedding to arguing with him over whether he might have been flirting with her lately.

Their noses bumped. They both laughed.

And then the laughter faded. She pulled back a little. They stared at each other.

He held her by the waist then. And she had her capable hands on his shoulders.

"Oh, Ethan," she whispered. "What is happening here?"

He thought about all the reasons he shouldn't be doing this. All the ways getting intimate with her would ruin everything.

And then he thought that if she really was leaving, well, it was ruined anyway. That he would have to learn to get along without her. That August, after she left him, when she went back to Midland, was going to be hell.

Might as well have something really good to remember when she was gone.

But would *she* want that? Something temporary? Something they would both walk away from when July came to an end?

Somehow, that didn't seem like Lizzie, to have a temporary fling. Especially not with him.

Because, seriously, he wasn't her kind of guy. Lizzie went more for the solid-citizen type. She went for the guy who was looking for the right woman to settle down with, to raise a family with.

Ethan liked his life the way it was. No strings. No commitments, lifetime or otherwise.

He said, "I don't know what's happening." And he realized he meant it. One moment, it all seemed so clear to him, that he should keep his hands off her, that getting intimate with Lizzie was the kind of uncharted territory he had no right to explore.

And then the next moment, he found himself thinking that he'd go nuts if he couldn't touch her, if he couldn't find out what it would feel like to kiss her.

"So...what should we do?" Her eyes were so green right then. So wide. And her mouth was soft, perfect for kissing.

And then he was thinking, well, why not? He'd already kissed her once.

And he really, really wanted to kiss her again.

"Ethan?" Her eyes searched his face. "I—"

"Shh. Don't talk. Not right now."

"Ethan..."

He took her mouth again. He simply could not resist. And she didn't pull away. She made a soft, surprised little sound. And then she surrendered—to him. To the moment. To...this thing between them that had always been one thing and now was becoming something else altogether.

Something magic. Something scary. Something he had never in a thousand years expected to happen with her, with Lizzie, who was the finest damn assistant he'd ever had, his favorite all-time cook and housekeeper. And most important of all, his best friend.

She kissed him back, reluctantly at first, and then with a lost little sigh as she gave in to him, to the moment. She parted her lips for him so he could taste her more deeply.

He could have gone on like that into next week. Holding Lizzie. Kissing her...

But too soon, she put her hands against his chest. She turned her mouth away from him. "Ethan..."

He knew he'd pushed her about as far as she was going to go. "All right." He loosened his hold, but couldn't quite bring himself to let go.

She did that for him, taking his wrists and peeling them away from the firm curve of her waist. Cradling his hands between hers, she held his gaze. "The more I think about this, the more I think it's not a direction you and I should be going."

"So don't think."

She laughed then, a wry sound. "Of course that would be your advice on the subject."

"I like to live in the moment."

"No kidding. But I really do think we need to...forget what just happened, forget it and move on."

He stepped back, giving her the space he knew she needed right then. And she let go of his hands. He echoed glumly, "Forget it and move on..."

Her gaze didn't waver. "That's what I said."

He didn't like the turn things were suddenly taking. He didn't like it at all. "Oh, come on, Lizzie. I kissed you. You kissed me back. We can't un-remember that."

"We can pretend to. We can *behave* as though it never happened."

He wished she was joking, but he knew that she wasn't. "That's what you want, really? To pretend it never happened?"

"That's what I want, yes."

He realized he was furious with her. So he spoke very softly, with cold, precise care. "Well, all right, then. Fine with me. You got it. I'll give you exactly what you want."

About a half an hour later, they went up to the resort in their separate cars.

The morning was similar to the day before. They met with Grant. Ethan had questions and Grant answered them. There was more in-depth study of the accounts, more discussion of what areas needed more investment and where corners might be cut.

Lizzie did her job and wished she were anywhere else but there, near Ethan. She was just too...aware of him now. She kept thinking of how lovely it had felt, to be held in his arms. How tender and perfect his kisses had been. She kept doing exactly what she had told him she wouldn't do: remembering in aching, perfect detail, every sigh, every touch, every word that had passed between them at breakfast.

He'd been right, of course. She couldn't un-remember that she had kissed him. And it was going to be close to impossible to pretend that nothing between them had changed.

Plus, he was seriously pissed off at her. Oh, he was civil enough. He treated her with calm professionalism, just like any good boss would. But she knew that closed-off look in those dark eyes of his. He was angry at her for wanting to put the events of the morning behind them.

At least Grant didn't seem to notice that anything was different. Lizzie was grateful for that.

The morning seemed to last forever. But finally, at 11:30, she had her chance to escape. She left the men in the conference room and drove back down the mountain into town.

In town, she found a parking lot tucked into the corner where Thunder Canyon Road turned sharply and became Main Street. The lot serviced both a motel called the Wander-On Inn, and the Hitching Post, the bar where Ethan had attended Corey's bachelor party. Lizzie parked in the lot and walked to the restaurant.

It was a cool, sunny day. Perfect for a stroll. The buildings were old, mostly of brick. They'd probably been there since the turn of the previous century, and then refitted to make the current shops and stores that lined the cute, old-timey street.

She found the restaurant a couple of blocks down from where she'd left the car. It had *The Tottering Teapot* painted in green-and-pink flowing script on the wide front window, which was hung with old-fashioned lace curtains on café rods.

Inside, the tables were all different sizes, covered in antique lace tablecloths, no two the same. Even the chairs were all different shapes and styles, as though the place had been furnished from any number of yard and estate sales.

Petite, pretty Allaire Traub sat at a table for five near the far wall with one other woman, a brightly dressed strawberry blonde, at her side. Allaire signaled Lizzie over.

"You made it." She jumped to her feet and pulled out a chair. "Lizzie, this is Tori McFarlane."

Lizzie greeted Tori and took the chair Allaire had offered. A few minutes later, Haley Cates joined them. Haley ran a youth program called ROOTS in a storefront Lizzie recalled passing on her way to the restaurant. The women explained that they usually met Mondays for lunch. But this week, Allaire couldn't get away until Tuesday, so here they were.

"You're welcome to join us," said Haley, "right here at the Tottering Teapot, most Mondays at lunchtime."

"Consider it an open invitation," Allaire added with a glowing smile.

They ordered from the hand-lettered menus, and their sandwiches arrived on beautiful old plates in floral-and-blue Delft and gold-leaf patterns. The dishes and flatware didn't match any more than the tablecloths or chairs did. Every piece was different. The place was cozy, friendly and unpretentious. Lizzie felt instantly welcome there.

She liked the three women, too. She learned how Haley had married a former town bad boy, Marlon Cates. She also found out that Allaire was an art teacher and Tori taught English. Tori and Connor planned to stay in Thunder

Canyon through the next school year so that Connor's son, CJ, could finish high school at TC High.

"But McFarlane House headquarters are back east," Tori said. "We'll probably make Philadelphia our home base as soon as CJ's in college."

Allaire and Haley swore they weren't letting Tori go. But Tori only smiled at them and said she loved them dearly and would be back to visit often.

Rose Traub had told Allaire about Lizzie's plans to open a bakery in Midland—and Allaire had turned right around and told all her friends.

"And we've been thinking…" Allaire announced with a knowing grin.

Haley finished for her "…that you ought to stay here and open your bakery in Thunder Canyon."

Lizzie laughed. "You know, Erin said the same thing Saturday afternoon, when I delivered her wedding cake to the resort."

"Well, you ought to listen to Erin," said Haley. "We really need someone like you, someone approachable and easy to get to know. Someone we like."

"Someone dependable," added Allaire.

Tori said, "The guy who owns La Boulangerie—the bakery a block down, at Nugget and Main?—he's a great baker. Croissants you would kill for, no kidding. But he's not a friendly guy. And then look what happened last week? He just up and vanished without a word to anyone. Luckily, you were here to save the day for Erin. But the bakery's been shut up tight ever since. That leaves the doughnut shop in New Town, the one Starbucks on North Main and that other chain bakery in the mall. Old Town needs a real artisan bakery."

"He's French, the runaway baker down the street," said

Haley with a frown—and then caught herself. "Not that there's anything wrong with being French."

Lizzie laughed. "I'm glad you qualified that. My dear *maman* was French. And my dad was of French extraction."

"Well, the baker down the street was not a happy Frenchman," said Tori. "I think he had a girlfriend for a while, though, didn't he? He seemed a little happier then."

"That's right," said Hayley. "That pretty, dark-haired woman. French, too, as I remember. I wonder if she went with him…."

"No clue," said Allaire. "But you, Lizzie, you're fun *and* talented. And clearly super-dependable, too. Everyone knows that Ethan is going to be lost without you. You've totally spoiled him, and that's a fact."

Ethan. Just the mention of his name made her feel sad and tense and worried. And a little bit breathless, too. The swirl of emotions was pretty overwhelming.

Oh, what was she thinking to let him kiss her—and then to go and kiss him right back?

She said, rather feebly, "Oh, I'm sure he'll be fine."

Allaire made a low, disbelieving sound. "Corey once said that Ethan couldn't keep an assistant until you came along. They all ended up falling in love with him, pining over him all day instead of doing their work."

"I'd say that's something of an exaggeration." Hah. And now she was just like all the others. Feeling breathless and tortured at the very mention of his name.

"Well, I know he'll miss you," Allaire said. She went on, "And I mean it. If you decided to stay here, you would never regret it. Your bakery would be a success from the first day you opened the doors for business. You can count on us to make sure of that."

Tori and Hayley both nodded enthusiastic agreement. Of course, Ethan's cousin and her friends were just being welcoming. But still, Lizzie found the wild idea kind of appealing. She did like Thunder Canyon. The country was spectacular and everyone was so friendly and easy to get along with.

But no, her plans were already made. "Sorry. I'm flattered, but I'm a Midland, Texas, girl through and through."

"Think it over," said Allaire. "That's all we're asking."

"Yeah." Tori sipped her tea. "There's no law that says you can't change your mind."

After she said goodbye to the others outside the restaurant, Lizzie had half an hour before Ethan would expect her at the resort. She was not in a hurry to spend the rest of the day at his side valiantly pretending nothing had changed between them.

So she dawdled a little. She wandered farther down the block to get a look at the Frenchman's deserted bakery.

What could it hurt, after all, to look?

La Boulangerie had a storefront much like the one that housed the Tottering Teapot: an old brick building with wide showcase windows in front and a glass-topped door of heavy dark wood. Lizzie pressed her face against the window glass to see inside.

It was nice in there, with wide-planked floors, a few tables so people could eat their treats right there, lots of shelving, the usual long glass-cased counters. She admired the gorgeous old espresso machine and a quality bread slicer. She'd really love to get a look in the back, see what the prep space was like....

Just out of curiosity, she took the alley between the bakery and the building next door. Through a window on the side wall, she got a limited view of steel tables, of rolling racks, of a couple of handsome-looking proofers—sealed steel boxes that kept yeast dough at optimum warmth and humidity. She saw two high-capacity ovens and the shiny steel doors of refrigeration units. The floor mixer was a Hobart and there was a nice, big counter mixer as well, also a Hobart, which was arguably best of the best when it came to professional mixers.

She went on to the back, where she found parking. Plenty of it. There was a rear entrance with a steel door. No windows back there, not on the ground floor. But double-hung windows gleamed high up the brick wall. An iron fire escape zigzagged down from the roof, with a landing under the windows.

Was there an apartment up there? She smiled to herself. A baker got up early. Life would be easier if she lived above her shop.

And what would that be like, to live above her very own bakery on Main Street in Thunder Canyon, Montana?

Was it possible that the runaway French baker might be planning to sell? If he hoped to come back to town and pick up where he'd left off, she wished him a whole lot of luck. People weren't happy with the way he'd behaved.

And if he did end up selling, well, she could probably get the business and all the equipment at a really good price. Quality equipment was so expensive. The Hobart Legacy floor mixer alone would cost her upward of fifteen-thousand dollars, new....

And then she shook her head.

It was just a pleasant fantasy, really, nothing she would ever actually do. In Midland, she had her eye on a couple of locations. She had to admit, though, that neither of those was quite as attractive as this one.

But still, the whole idea was to re-create the family bakery she had lost. And that bakery belonged in Midland, Texas.

Plus, if she did decide to relocate here, she'd be living

in the same small town as Ethan. That would be difficult. She'd been kind of counting on cutting it clean with him, on giving them both some serious distance while they each grew accustomed to life on their own.

Life on their own.

Sheesh. As if they were an old married couple or something—an old married couple calling it quits.

She glanced at her watch.

Yikes. Time had gotten away from her. She was going to be late getting back to the resort. So much for daydreaming—and trying to put off being around Ethan again, to delay the upcoming afternoon of playing it as if everything was business as usual.

When, in reality, it had all gone so wrong.

Ethan sat in the comfortable leather conference-room chair and tried to pay attention to Grant's really excellent PowerPoint presentation. He had a tall glass of mint-garnished iced tea at his elbow served by Grant's assistant right after they'd returned from a nice lunch in the Lounge. Ethan also had a pen and a notebook close at hand, should he feel the need to jot down a note. Hell, he had his PDA right there and could use it if the pen ran out of ink.

He really did *not* need for Lizzie to be there.

It was just that she was *supposed* to be there. But she wasn't. She was late. And Lizzie was never late.

Until today.

Ethan didn't like it. He'd given her two full hours for lunch. She'd agreed to be back at the resort and on hand in the conference room by 1:30. It was now 1:45. Annoyance moved through him, a prickly, uneasy feeling, like bees buzzing under his skin.

Was she all right? Had she been in an accident or something?

The very thought that something bad might have happened to her scared him to death. So he decided not to think about that.

No. She was fine. He was sure of it. He focused on his annoyance with her for being late, in order to keep from imagining that she might be in trouble.

It was…the principle of the thing. He paid her a fortune—especially if you counted that bonus she was getting at the end of July when she left him high and dry to go bake cupcakes for a living—and the least she could do was to be there, ready to work if he needed her for the too-short time she remained in his employ.

Grant began clicking through a series of images showing construction of the just-completed golf course, which had been started three years ago and put on hold for twenty-four months when the economy soured. "But we finished work on it this year, as soon as the snow gave us a break. And the grand opening two weeks ago brought in golfers from all over the country. It's not a large course, but it's a beauty and it really is a necessity for a year-round resort destination."

The conference-room door opened silently. Ethan wouldn't even have noticed it if he hadn't had his head turned so he could see the door from the corner of his eye.

Lizzie slipped in.

Grant sent her a smile. "Lizzie."

She gave Clifton a small wave and took her place at the long table.

Ethan let his gaze glide dismissively past her. "About time."

He was going to have a word with her about her lateness—this evening at dinner, as a matter of fact.

Yeah, okay. He'd been thinking he would eat out, get away from the house and the tension between them, maybe try the Hitching Post. He could get a beer and burger there. Plus, he might meet someone pretty and friendly and available, someone who wouldn't make a federal case out of a few innocent kisses.

But on second thought, no. He'd eat at home and he'd get it clear with Lizzie that as long as she was his employee, he expected her to be on time.

At four, as they were wrapping up for the day, Grant asked Ethan if he planned to be back in town week after next.

When Ethan said yes, Grant suggested they go for that golf-cart and horseback tour of the property that Connor had mentioned the day before. "How about if I set it up for Tuesday, the twenty-first? Be here at the offices, dressed for riding, at nine. We can change the date if that doesn't work for Connor. I'm sure he would really like to go along."

"The twenty-first is fine," Ethan said. "But I'm flexible. Let me know if another day would be better."

Grant promised he would. The men shook hands.

Ethan and Lizzie left the offices. Out in the parking lot, he made a point of not speaking to her. She didn't say a word to him, either. They got in their separate cars and headed down the mountain.

He almost went to the Hitching Post anyway. He could a use a drink in a friendly atmosphere. And then he could go home for dinner and tell Lizzie he didn't appreciate her wandering back to work whenever the mood suited her.

But he had some calls to make. He needed to touch base with his mom and with Roger, to check in with the Midland office and make confirmation calls to Helena and Great Falls. So they ended up caravanning to the house and pulling into the garage side by side.

In the house, she actually spoke to him. Coolly, without

so much as a hint of a smile. "Will you be eating dinner here tonight?"

"Yeah. Seven?"

"I'll have it ready."

"Good. I'd like a Maker's Mark, rocks, in my office at six-thirty."

"You got it."

He left her and went to his study, where he shut the door and picked up the phone.

After the calls, he took off his tie and undid the top buttons on his shirt and went over the spreadsheets Roger had emailed him from Midland.

Lizzie tapped on his door at six-thirty exactly.

"It's open," he said in a flat voice.

She brought in his drink and set it on a coaster by his desk blotter without once meeting his eyes. He waited to reach for it until, silently closing the door behind her, she left him alone again. Then he grabbed the glass, knocked back a healthy shot and hoisted his tooled boots up on the side of his desk. The whiskey burned a satisfying trail down his throat. He braced the glass on his stomach and studied his boots. Usually, kicking back at the end of the day with his boots up was a very satisfying moment for Ethan.

Not today, though. And all because of the tall, wild-haired muffin maker in the kitchen.

He had another fine, smooth sip and he asked himself, was he overdoing the lord-of-the-manor routine just a little?

Okay, yeah. Maybe.

But damn it, now he not only had to accept that she really was deserting him, but he also had to let her go without going where he'd just discovered he really wanted to go with her—namely, the nearest bed.

Five years she'd been with him, day in and day out. And until a few days ago, he'd never had the slightest clue that he wanted her. That was pretty damn strange, if you thought about it. Pretty…unsettling.

But still, he was willing to work with the strangeness of it all. He was willing to get past the unsettling nature of the whole thing. He could just accept that he wanted Lizzie. It was a fact and he was ready to deal with it.

But not Lizzie. Oh, no.

Lizzie wasn't willing. Uh-uh. Lizzie had told him right to his face that she wasn't kissing him again. She wasn't… going in that direction with him. She even wanted him to *un*-remember that he'd kissed her in the first place.

It was insulting. Seriously. He wasn't a bad guy. As a rule, women *liked* him. They *really* liked him.

Okay, he knew he wasn't Lizzie's type, the looking-to-settle-down type. But still. She could make an exception just this once, couldn't she?

After all, she wanted him, too. There was no faking the way she'd kissed him that morning—and she wasn't the kind who faked it anyway. Why couldn't she just let nature take its course? It could be really good for both of them.

Ethan swung his boots to the floor and stood from the high-backed leather swivel chair. Enough of this sitting here, stewing over this whole annoying situation.

He had a few things to say to her. And now was as good a time as any to say them.

Chapter Seven

"Lizzie," Ethan said.

Lizzie felt a shiver down her spine. She had her back to him. She paused in the act of slicing sweet peppers for the salad and waited for what he was going to say next.

But he didn't say anything. Only her name, in that low, rough tone that brought to mind some hungry wild animal, growling with his lips curled back. A wild animal showing sharp, mean teeth in that moment right before he went for the throat.

"What can I get for you?" she asked brightly, setting down her paring knife and turning to face him where he lounged in the doorway. He had one big arm crossed over his middle. The other was straight at his side, his half-finished drink dangling from his fingers. She tried again, "Refresh your drink?"

He just looked at her, a look that managed to be both furious and lazy at once.

She refused to let him see that he was getting to her. Cheerfully, she informed him, "Dinner's almost ready." The prime rib was out of the oven, resting on the cooktop. She had the potatoes whipped and the green beans buttered and waiting in a covered serving dish.

He raised the glass, deftly shifting it so that he cradled it in his big palm. And he took a slow, thoughtful sip. "You were late today, after lunch."

She had known that was coming. "Yeah." She grabbed the hand towel on the counter beside her, wiped her hands, set it back down again. "I'm really sorry. I let the time get away from me."

"Two hours wasn't enough for lunch?"

She let a long pause elapse before answering that one. "Two hours was more than enough. I appreciated the extra time. I should have made it back when I said I would. I really do apologize. It won't happen again."

"See that it doesn't."

Okay, now he was really starting to annoy her. She asked with excruciating civility, "Ethan, how many times have I been late back from lunch—or at all—in the years that I've worked for you?"

He sipped his drink again, then studied the glass. "You know, I think I *will* have another drink."

It was too much. "Will you please have the courtesy to answer my question first?"

He shrugged. "You're right. You're never late. Until today."

"I'm so pleased you're aware of that. And I have apologized for today. Can we be done now with beating that particular dead horse?"

"Sure." He held out his glass.

They glared at each other. It was such a tacky power play, his insisting that she get his drink. As if he couldn't stroll on over to the wet bar in the family room and get his own damn refill.

But fine. All right. She *was* his housekeeper, and getting his drinks was her job. With a hard snort of disgust, she marched over to him and took the glass. He remained there, lounging in the doorway.

"Excuse me," she said in a tone that made it more than clear she would love to throw what was left of that drink right in his smug, too-handsome face.

"Oh. Sorry." He straightened enough that she could slip past him.

She marched into the family room, poured him another and returned to the kitchen, where he had yet to budge from the doorway. "Here you go."

"Thanks." He took the drink.

She eased around him again and returned to the counter, intent on serving him his meal and then leaving him alone to have his prime rib by himself. She picked up her paring knife and glared at the red mini-pepper waiting on the cutting board.

Behind her, he hadn't moved. And this was ridiculous. A farce. She wasn't putting up with this treatment for one more minute.

She slapped the knife down, turned on him again and folded her arms tightly across her stomach. "Ethan, you're being a complete ass. You know that, right?"

He scowled at her. "Oh, great. Now I'm an ass."

"Yes, you are." She softened her tone a fraction. "And being an ass is not like you. As a rule, you're a good, kind man. A fair man."

He had nothing to say to that. He only straightened from the doorway and went to the table, where he yanked out his usual chair and dropped into it. She'd already put his place setting there. He sipped his drink and set the glass on the corner of the place mat. His was the only setting. He gestured toward the empty spot across the table. "What is that?"

She only stared at him.

And he said, "Look, I get it, okay. I finally get that there's nothing I can do to keep you from leaving. But I don't get why you won't sit down at the damn table and eat your dinner across from me. That's just…well, that's plain mean, Lizzie. You know that it is."

She felt sorry for him suddenly, all her righteous anger with him drained away. She said gently, "Ethan, come on. The way you've been behaving today, why would I want to sit down and share a meal with you? Trying to eat my dinner with you sitting there glaring at me, it's a surefire prescription for indigestion, you've got to know that."

He slumped back in the chair. "Okay. All right. I'll behave, I promise. Just…set yourself a place, and please, can we eat?"

She studied his face for a long time, feeling all tender and sorry and sad. And then, finally, she nodded. "Just a few minutes."

"Great." A weary smile. "Thanks."

So she finished cutting up the salad and brought it to the table. He carved the roast for her and brought over the meat platter as she put the au jus in a gravy boat and set out the green beans.

The buzzer went off to let her know the yeast rolls were ready. She transferred them to a breadbasket. "Wine?"

He shook his head. "You?"

"Not tonight."

They sat down, passed the food to each other and ate in silence for several minutes.

Finally, with care, she set down her fork. "Ethan…"

He looked up from his plate. "What? I'm behaving."

Fondness washed through her. "It's not about that."

"Then what?"

"I just want to say, in case it might be better for you, that I don't *have* to stay on until the end of July. If you're finding it hard to…I don't know, be around me now, it's okay. I understand. I could go back to Midland and see about finding you a new assistant. Or I could find one for you here. Or I could just, well, go."

He set down his fork, too. He sat very still, watching her, his eyes so dark, his expression somber. Then, very softly, he said, "No. Please. Don't go. Stay. I don't want to give you up until I have to. And don't…find me your replacement. There is no one who can replace you."

She suddenly felt misty-eyed. "Oh, Ethan…"

"I'll deal with the problem when I have to, when you're gone. But until then, do me a favor. Just keep on as we have been, help me to get started here in Thunder Canyon. That's what I want for now, that's what works best for me."

There was a definite pressure at the back of her throat, the tightness of tears rising. She swallowed them down. "It's meant so much, really. To work for you. To…be your friend. When you first hired me, I hardly knew where my next meal was coming from. I'd gone off to college secure that I had a home and the family business to return to. But when I got back, it was all gone. I was so scared, Ethan. For myself. For my poor, lost father. But you gave me a job. You gave me…a chance. And I got to find out how really capable I am. And not only that, you bailed my dad out of jail, you made it so he could get some kind of life back when I was pretty much certain he would never find his way to anything resembling peace or stability. And when he died, you were the one who was there for me. I *am* grateful to you, in a thousand ways. But I have to live my life for me, you know?"

His Adam's apple bounced as he swallowed. "I know."

"I can't stay with you if you're just going to be mean and cold to me. As much as I care about you, I'm not up for taking a lot of punishment from you for the next seven weeks. That wouldn't be good for either of us."

"I hear you," he said, his voice low and rough. "I was out of line and I know it. I'm having a little trouble getting it in my head that there's no way to change your mind about going."

"I know."

"And then there's the rest of it," he said gruffly. She took his meaning: the sudden, surprising attraction between them. "Seeing you in this different way. It has me all turned around sideways, with my head spinning."

"I know the feeling," she confessed in near-whisper.

He picked up a yeast roll from the basket, broke it in half, met her gaze across the table. "I'm used to being interested in more...willing women."

She laughed then. "Oh, Ethan." And then she didn't feel like laughing at all. She felt that little curl of heat down low in her belly, just from staring into those beautiful eyes of his. "That would be too difficult for me. I don't do casual intimate relationships, or at least I never have. And I don't feel comfortable trying that out now."

His chuckle was lacking in humor. "And I *only* do casual."

"Exactly." She gazed at him and he stared back at her and all at once, she was recalling one of the many times he'd broken up with his latest girlfriend because he said the woman was getting too serious.

"I don't do serious," he'd confided in Lizzie over a cup of decaf the night of the breakup. "I never will."

She'd rolled her eyes and told him to wait. Someday

he'd meet someone really special and he'd want to get serious.

He laughed and said that was never going to happen. "Some men just don't do well in captivity. I'm one of those."

She got annoyed with him then, for equating a real relationship with captivity. She punched him in the arm and called him a bad name. He only laughed and then asked her reproachfully, "Lizzie, if I can't tell you the truth, who can I tell it to?"

"Lizzie?"

She blinked and brought herself back to the present. "Sorry. Just thinking."

"I won't be an ass again."

"I'm so glad to hear that."

"I'll keep it friendly, but not *too* friendly. Will that work?"

"Yes, it will." She forced a smile.

They picked up their forks and continued the meal.

A few minutes later, he said, "We should leave by eight tomorrow morning. We've got a ten-o'clock meeting with a couple of land brokers in Helena."

"I'll be ready."

"It's a week and a half of being mostly on the move."

"I know, Ethan."

"So we're good, then? We're set?"

"We are, yes."

"Fair enough."

They spent Wednesday and Thursday in Helena and Friday and Saturday in Great Falls.

Sunday, they moved east. Ethan was buying up mineral rights in the more promising areas of the Bakken Shale, a large area of oil-rich shale land that covered over two-hundred-thousand square miles in Montana, North Dakota and Canada. A lot of the rights were already claimed, but if a company didn't make use of the rights, they expired. Ethan was on the trail of some of those expired leases, plus trying to get his hands on leases yet to be bought.

He also wanted to see some of the newer horizontal extraction equipment in action. They spent more than one day out in the middle of nowhere among giant, loud machines. She teased him about that. There was plenty of state-of-the-art equipment to see in Texas, after all. They also spent some nights in some not-so-attractive motel rooms in tiny towns with limited lodging choices.

But Ethan was in his element. It seemed to her that he was happier than she'd ever seen him. He loved being out in the wide-open, windy expanses of northeastern Montana, wearing old boots, a wrinkled shirt, a faded pair of Wranglers and a sweat-stained straw Resistol cowboy hat. He'd always dreamed of being a real, old-time oilman like his dad had been, back when the industry was wide-open and everyone thought the supply of black crude would never run dry.

One night, at the Golden Lariat Motel on the outskirts of a tiny town called Coyote Creek near the border of North Dakota, they sat in molded plastic chairs out by the pool after a really bad dinner at a local greasy spoon. The pool was empty. Not that it really mattered. The wind was blowing and it was too cold for a swim anyway.

"Such a scenic spot," she said drily, shivering a little in her light jacket, staring across the deserted highway at the lonely-looking gas station on the other side.

He hoisted his dusty boots onto a spare plastic chair. "This is the life, Lizzie." He sent her his cockiest grin. And then his expression changed. He gazed into the distance.

"Being CFO? It wasn't working for me anymore. I was beginning to feel like I was suffocating. A man can't spend his whole life waiting for the older generation to retire, you know?" He sent her a glance.

"I get it," she said. "And I think it's great, that you're moving on. I really do. I think it's the best thing for you, to make your own place in the company—on your own terms."

He was watching her. "I'm glad you're here with me. For now, at least."

"Me, too." As she said it, she realized it was true.

His slow smile made her heart kind of stumble inside her chest. "Feel free to change your mind and stay."

"Not going to happen." She said it softly. A little bit breathlessly.

"You're a damn stubborn woman, Lizzie Landry."

"And you, Ethan Traub, are a pigheaded man."

He gestured at the dusty, empty pool, at the deserted highway and the endless, dry land around them, at a lonely tumbleweed bouncing down the center line. "I can't believe you want to give up all this."

She frowned. "Are you going to start in on that again?"

"I'm persistent. It's why I succeed at most things I do."

"You won't change my mind. It doesn't matter what you say, or how much money you offer me."

"I really hate that I've started to believe you."

"Only started?"

He didn't rise to that challenge. Instead, he asked, "And what about when I want one of your chocolate-chip muffins? Or a strawberry-rhubarb pie?"

"You'll have to have them shipped up from Midland. And it will cost you."

"Ouch. That's cold." But he didn't look especially upset about it.

He really was making his peace with the changes between them. Slowly. Reluctantly, he was letting her go.

She told herself that was for the best, that his acceptance of her leaving was what she wanted.

But her heart felt heavy suddenly. Weighted with the coming loss.

Of Ethan. Of the special relationship they shared as colleagues. As friends.

As...

Okay, she might as well admit it: as possibly so much more.

Mon Dieu, as her dear *maman* might have said. Where was she going with this? She'd been after him for months to accept that she was leaving. She was finally getting somewhere with that, finally seeing the light at the end of the tunnel, seeing the day coming when she could move on and he could wish her well as she left him.

She should be pleased. But instead, she was feeling droopy and dejected about getting exactly what she wanted.

It made no sense. Last week, she'd called *him* an ass. Well, who was being the ass now?

"Okay, Lizzie," he said in a low, teasing voice that played dangerous music on every one of her nerve endings. "What's happening inside that head of yours?"

She met his waiting eyes. Oh, she did long to tell him—that she wanted her bakery and she wanted *him,* too. She wanted to stay with him. And she *needed* to go. That she didn't do casual when it came to the man-woman thing—and yet, she was actually considering making an exception in his case.

Uh-uh. No good was going to come of telling him all that. It would only confuse him all over again. He didn't need that.

Neither of them needed that.

"Just watching the empty highway," she said. "Waiting for something exciting to roll by."

He laughed, a low, sexy rumble of sound. "Liar."

"Look." She pointed toward the two-lane road. "Another tumbleweed."

He didn't look. He kept right on staring at her. "You want to change your mind—about anything—you be sure and let me know."

Lizzie did nothing of the kind.

Not that night, or any of the remaining nights that they were on the road. They worked all day. At night, they had dinner in diners and chain restaurants. They were joined by any number of interesting characters, by crusty ranchers and land brokers. They even met up with a few current TOI employees, landmen Ethan had sent on ahead to start lining up the mineral-rights possibilities—a landman being a professional who secures oil and gas leases, checks legal titles and attempts to repair title defects so that drilling can begin.

After each day's work, they retired to their separate motel rooms. The next morning they got up, drove to the next meeting and did it all over again.

They returned to Thunder Canyon Sunday around noon, after ten and a half days on the road. Ethan was pleased with all they had accomplished. He was already talking about getting equipment in place and hiring rig crews for the leases he was acquiring in the most promising areas.

He went to his office. Lizzie unpacked, whipped the house into shape and left to buy groceries. Ethan appeared in the garage when she returned and helped her carry everything in.

"Don't cook tonight," he instructed, as he hauled in the last armful of bags.

"Why not?" She'd been kind of looking forward to her own cooking after the endless chain of diners and greasy spoons they'd been eating in.

"I got a call from Allaire. While we were on the road, we missed the second-annual summer-kickoff barbecue last weekend at the Rib Shack. Allaire invited us there for dinner tonight to kind of make up for our missing the big event."

"Where?"

"The Rib Shack, up at the resort. It'll be a family thing. Allaire and DJ, Dax and Shandie." Dax Traub was DJ's older brother by a year. Shandie was Dax's wife. "And that's not all," Ethan said. "Dillon and Erika are coming. And Corey and Erin are back from their honeymoon, so they'll be there, too. Allaire says they're all looking forward to seeing us."

Lizzie paused in the act of putting lettuce in the crisper. *Us,* he'd said so easily. As if the two of them were a couple or something.

But they weren't. And they never would be. And she really, really needed to remember that.

The problem was, lately, it was getting harder and harder to keep in mind that in a matter of weeks, she would be in Midland and he would be here. And it was very possible, unless he happened to come down to Texas and drop in at her bakery, that she would never see him again.

Never see him again.

The words echoed in her mind. They did not make a pleasant sound.

"Lizzie, did you hear a single word I just said?"

She pushed the crisper drawer shut, pulled her head out

of the refrigerator and gently shut the door. "Of course I heard you. The Rib Shack for dinner."

He seemed hurt. "You should see your face. What? You don't like DJ's ribs?"

It wasn't the ribs that had her looking glum. It was… all that stuff they'd promised each other they were putting behind them. It was losing him, which she was beginning to understand she actually dreaded in the worst way—losing him to live her lifelong dream.

Losing him. Hah. As if she'd ever even had him.

She knew very well she hadn't. Not really. Just because they worked together and lived in the same house and were good buddies, well, that wasn't the same thing at all as them being *truly* together, the way a man and a woman could be. Like Allaire and DJ. Like Dillon and Erika.

Like Corey and Erin.

Like her mom and dad had been all those years ago.

She forced a grin that only wobbled a little. "Are you kidding? DJ's ribs are the best. Melt-in-your-mouth tender. That special secret sauce to die for…"

"Lizzie…" He came to her and put his hands on her shoulders. It was the first time he'd touched her on purpose since the night she called him an ass and he'd promised to change his attitude. The first touch in days and days.

And it felt downright wonderful.

Those lean, strong hands of his, clasping her shoulders. The warmth of him. And he must have showered while she was out shopping. He smelled so fresh and clean. And she'd always loved that aftershave he wore….

"You're trembling." He said it softly and his eyes were full of warmth, full of hope.

And promises—no, not of forever.

But of a glorious, magical, perfect *right now*.

"It's nothing," she told him on a whisper that trembled just as her body did.

"And now you're lying to me. Again. The way you did that night by the empty pool at the glamorous Golden Lariat Motel."

"Oh, Ethan."

"I knew what you were thinking that night. I know...a lot about you, Lizzie. More than you give me credit for."

"It...hurts, that's all." She shut her eyes, let out a groan. "Oh, I shouldn't have said that." And then she met his gaze again. She never wanted to look away.

"What hurts?"

"Don't make me say any more, Ethan."

"I'm not making you say—or do—anything. And you know I'm not."

She gulped to clear the clenching of her throat. "I... It's only that sometimes I think about how much I'm going to miss you. It hurts to think about it. It hurts a lot."

The light of triumph flashed in his eyes. "So don't go."

Step back, she thought. *Pull away. Do it now.*

But she didn't.

Instead, she did what she'd sworn she wouldn't. She told him the truth. "You know I have to go at the end of July. It wouldn't work now, for me to stay on, even if I didn't have dreams of my own to make happen. You're in my heart, Ethan. I couldn't go on, just working for you, with us being friends. It wouldn't be enough for me. Not now. Not anymore."

He touched her face, a caress that sent another warm shiver sliding through her. He whispered her name. And then he gathered her close and wrapped his arms around her.

And she let him, even though he hadn't said that she

was in *his* heart, too. Even though he hadn't said, *Stay, Lizzie. We'll work it out, you and me.*

Really, why should he say that? She knew him, after all. And by his own declaration, he wasn't the kind of man a woman counted on for a lifetime.

Still, she sighed in relief and joy, just at the feel of his big body pressed close, of his arms so tight around her.

And when he tipped up her chin and lowered his mouth to hers, she only sighed some more and welcomed his kiss.

Oh, my. Oh, yes…

Kissing Ethan in the kitchen.

It could easily become a habit for her.

It felt so good, so right. So exciting, so exactly as a man's kiss should feel. Why was it that no other man's kiss had thrilled her quite like Ethan's did?

He had a way of holding her in those big arms of his, a way of slanting his mouth just so, a way of tempting her to open—and that tongue of his. Really. There ought to be a law against a tongue like that. So clever, so…skilled. So very, very good at arousing her, at making her think how lovely it would be to fall into the nearest bed with him.

To stay there for the rest of the day and all of the night.

Her body felt hot and hungry. Needful in the most delicious way. And she couldn't resist pressing herself even closer, feeling more than she should have of how much he wanted her.

The man was an artist when it came to kissing.

And why shouldn't he be? asked the faint voice of reason somewhere way in the back of her desire-addled mind. *He's certainly had enough practice.*

That did it—just reminding herself of all of the girl-friends he'd had. Of the trail of broken hearts he'd left behind him in Texas.

She leaned back in his arms, breaking the sweet, end-less kiss.

His long, thick black lashes lifted and he looked at her. His lips were soft from kissing her. And his eyes were heavy-lidded. He asked, gruffly, "Second thoughts? Again?"

She gave him a bright, determined smile. "Sorry. I had a moment of weakness there. My bad."

Gently, he put her away from him. And then he let her go. She tried not to feel the loss of his touch too acutely.

He said, "I'm not going to make the same mistake again."

She didn't follow. "Mistake?"

"I'm not going to act like a jerk or get angry with you. I like you. So much, Lizzie. You're my friend. A good friend, steady, honest and true. And I admire the hell out of you, I really do."

"Uh. Thanks. I think."

"And I want you. I want you so bad. But I'm not going to die if I don't have you." He winced. And then he actu-ally chuckled. "Even if right now, it feels like I might."

She didn't know what to say to that. And as it turned out, she didn't need to say anything.

He wasn't through talking. "I'm not going to be cranky. And I'm not going to be an ass. If it's meant to happen with us, it will. I just want you to know that I'm willing. More than willing."

"Well, Ethan, I kind of figured that out already."

"Good. Then we're on the same page with this."

"I need to think it over." The words were out before she even realized she would say them. They shocked her a little and she felt her cheeks coloring. Every day she was getting closer to taking the leap. To going for it.

To making love with Ethan.

Maybe, she found herself thinking, it wouldn't be such a bad thing to live in the moment for a change, to let down her guard a little. Really, did she *always* have to be looking ahead to the future, planning for what would happen next?

For five years now, since her dad lost the bakery—no, before that. For ten years, since her beloved *maman* had died so quickly and brutally of cancer, she'd been living her life with such strict care. She'd pushed herself constantly, denying the pleasures of the moment to create a stable future for herself, a future neither death nor a loved one's heartsick inattentiveness could ever steal from her.

She'd been most careful of all in the men she dated. There had been only a few and they'd all been good marriage material.

But where had all that carefulness gotten her? None of those cautiously chosen men had worked out for her, none had stolen her heart and left her breathless the way Ethan did.

Stolen her heart.

Oh, yes. He had. He truly had. Ethan Traub had stolen her heart. She should probably be angry about that. It wasn't as though he was giving her his heart in return.

But she wasn't angry. She forgave him totally. She could love him for who he was and leave it at that.

He asked, "Whatever happened to that banker you were dating—what was his name?"

She felt, at that moment, that he could actually see inside her mind, that he knew just what she was thinking. She answered flatly, "His name was Charles. Charles Smith. And it didn't work out."

"And the insurance salesman? And what about the guy who taught high-school geometry?"

She gave him a stern look. "Get to the point."

"They were all really nice, stable, trustworthy guys, weren't they?"

"Just say it, Ethan."

"Maybe it wouldn't hurt you to take a risk on a different kind of guy now and then, that's all."

She braced her fists on her hips and made a very unladylike snorting sound. "A risk with *you*. That's what you really mean, isn't it?" She was glaring at him, but it was only an act.

In her mind was the realization that she had reached the all-important crossroads in her life. She would have her bakery, just as she'd planned. And Ethan had accepted at last that it would happen, that he would have to let her go.

She was thinking, what could it hurt? To just…be with him, for a little while? To be with him and for once to let the future take care of itself?

He finally answered her question. "A risk with me is exactly what I'm suggesting. So if you decide you want to go for it, you let me know."

"I'll, um, keep you posted."

His smile was wry and genuine. "Hey, a guy can't ask for more."

Chapter Eight

At the Rib Shack up at the resort, black-and-white pictures of cowboys and weathered buildings hung on the walls, each one tinted a faint sepia color, bringing back a feeling of the old West. There was also a large mural that showed scenes from Thunder Canyon history. Grant Clifton had told them it was painted by Allaire.

"Smells good in here," said Ethan.

Lizzie grinned at him. They'd been to more than one Rib Shack together. "Always does." Like DJ's other locations, the place smelled of the famous Rib Shack sweet-and-tangy sauce. Her mouth watered in anticipation of a big helping of messy, to-die-for ribs.

Ethan put his arm around her. Lizzie felt that quick little flash of excitement, the one that sizzled along her nerve endings whenever he touched her lately.

And this time, as that thrill went through her, she realized that she was okay with it. She accepted it. Since that afternoon, they knew where they stood with each other. He wasn't going to push her, or be an ass because he couldn't have what he wanted from her. It was up to her to make up her mind if anything was going to happen between them.

Already, one of the long family-style tables was filled with Traubs. Allaire had saved them two seats. They sat down and greeted the newlyweds. Erin and Corey looked tanned, relaxed and happy.

The food, like the seating, was family-style, big platters of ribs and barbecued chicken to pass around, bowls of coleslaw, corn on the cob and mashed potatoes, baskets of biscuits and steak fries. They loaded up their plates, tucked napkins in their collars and dug in.

At DJ's, you didn't stand on ceremony. And nobody cared if there was secret sauce on your chin.

Lizzie had a great time.

There was lots of local news to share.

First, there was the gossip about the new rib place in town, LipSmackin' Ribs. It had opened recently in the New Town Mall. DJ had been by there already. "Just to have a look," he told them.

Shandie, Dax's wife, chuckled. "I'll bet your eyes about popped out of your head."

Erin was nodding. "I heard the waitresses wear dinky short skirts and tight T-shirts that show a lot of belly—shirts with big, red lips printed on the front."

"As in lip smackin'?" Dillon asked with a groan.

Dax teased his brother. "So, DJ, you worried about a little competition?"

"Not in the least," DJ scoffed. "Tight T-shirts and short skirts don't sell ribs. Take the word of an expert on the subject. It's all in the secret sauce."

A murmur of agreement went up from everyone at the table.

DJ also shared the news that the town's most famous crook, Arthur Swinton, had apparently died of a heart attack in prison. Arthur, long a fixture on the town council, had been embezzling from the town coffers for years, and had been caught only the year before—the same year he'd run for mayor against Grant's cousin Bo Clifton and been defeated.

"I hate to speak ill of the dead," said Dax. "But Arthur was such a weasel." He turned to DJ. "Plus, remember when he made that play for Mom?"

"Shh." Shandie, Dax's wife, sent a glance in the direction of her seven-year-old, Kayla, who was busy down the table spreading honey on a biscuit for DJ and Allaire's toddler, Alex. "Little pitchers have big ears."

Dax laughed. "Honey, you have to know Mom never gave Swinton the time of day."

"She was the greatest," DJ said.

"Yes, she was," Dax agreed. "You did not mess with Mom."

DJ went on with the story. "She slapped Arthur's face and told him she was a happily married woman. And even if she was a dried-up old maid, she wouldn't be saying yes to a skinny weasel like him."

Dax was still laughing. "And then she told Dad."

"Uh-oh," said Erika.

"You'd better believe that," said DJ. "Dad knocked him down a peg or two with a couple of well-placed hard rights to the jaw. I don't think Swinton ever got over being slapped in the face and told off by Mom—and beaten up by Dad."

Shandie shook her head. "Well, no matter what bad things he did, I hope the poor guy finds peace in the afterlife."

Dax grunted. "Not a chance. I have a feeling his ass is on fire about now."

"Dax!" Shandie made a show of bumping her husband with her shoulder. "That's enough."

He put his arm around her and kissed her cheek. "Your wish is always my command."

Allaire caught Lizzie's eye. "So will we see you tomorrow at the Tottering Teapot for lunch?"

Lizzie tipped her head toward Mr. Tall, Dark and Texan at her side. "Depends on whether the slave driver can spare me for an hour or two."

Ethan heaved a fake sigh. "It will be difficult, but I'll manage."

Lizzie grinned. "I'll be there."

"Great. Erin and Erika are coming, too."

Erika nodded.

Erin beamed. "We wouldn't miss it. I loved the Bahamas, but it's good to be home—and we can plan that girls' night out I promised you when you saved the day and baked my wedding cake."

"Girls' night out?" Shandie looked interested.

"I hope we're all invited to that," Allaire chimed in.

"Oh, absolutely," Erin told them.

Erika added, "The more, the merrier, I always say."

"We're thinking about maybe this Friday night, but we can firm it all up tomorrow."

"Can't wait," said Lizzie.

"Me, neither," said Erin. "It's going to be fun."

"Did you have a good time tonight?" Ethan asked Lizzie as they drove back down the mountain.

"I did."

"I think you like it here." His eyes gleamed through the

darkness of the cab, and then he turned his gaze back to the road again.

"I think I do, yes." She gave him a smile.

They rode the rest of the way in silence.

At the house, she asked him if he wanted coffee or a last beer.

He gave her a crooked smile. "If I do, I'll get it myself. You are officially excused for the evening."

It was so strange, the feeling she had right then. Kind of sad and let down. He was only being thoughtful. She knew he didn't mean it as a rejection. And he certainly had a right to a little time to himself if he wanted it.

How many evenings in the years she had worked for him had he said he was fine on his own and didn't need anything more from her that night?

Hundreds, certainly. It was no big deal.

It was only that she had become accustomed lately to his constant attention. He'd been chasing her, spending every minute he could with her. And while he was chasing her, she'd told herself that she wished he would stop.

And now, true to his word that afternoon, he *had* stopped. And she wished that he hadn't.

Which was silly and unreasonable and counterproductive.

Still, it was how she felt.

Because I'm in love with him. Because he holds my heart...

Ugh. Really. She was going to have to buck up a little here. She had some big plans for herself. She was reaching a major long-term goal. And turning into a ball of sentimental mush over Ethan Traub?

No, not in the plan.

"Well, all right," she told him in a voice that made her proud, a voice that in no way betrayed the disappointment in her heart. "See you tomorrow."

She went to her rooms, where she drew a hot bath and soaked for an hour.

The water was soothing. Still, when she climbed from the tub, she just didn't feel much like sleeping. She put on an old pair of sweats and sat on the still-made bed and channel surfed.

Nothing caught her interest. So she picked up the phone and called a girlfriend in Midland. They talked for twenty minutes, about how the girlfriend was getting along in her new job, and about how Lizzie was doing way up there in Montana.

When she hung up, she felt even more on edge and dissatisfied than before. She sat there staring at the dark eye of the TV, thinking how her friend in Midland seemed like a casual acquaintance now. Really, she had more of a rapport with Allaire and Erin, with Erika and Tori McFarlane, than she did with a woman she'd known since she was in her teens.

She supposed it was her fault, for letting her life get so filled up with Ethan, for letting him become the center of her world, her boss at work and at home, and also her best friend.

"Ugh." She tossed both the remote and the phone down on the bed. Maybe a little chamomile tea would help her sleep.

She put on her flip-flops and went out to the kitchen, which was quiet—dark, except for the soft glow of the under-counter lights. Had Ethan gone out? She told herself she was not, under any circumstances, going to check the garage to see if his car was there.

That would just be too needy and pitiful for words.

Instead, she brewed her tea without turning on the overhead lights and went back to her room, where she sipped slowly and congratulated herself on not taking even one step down the short hallway to the inside garage entrance.

It wasn't until she turned off her bedroom light that she noticed the muted glow out on the back deck. She couldn't resist stealing a peek through the blinds: Ethan. He was sitting out there in a chaise lounge with a beer in his hand. The dim deck light didn't reveal much, just the shape of his body, stretched out in the chaise. She couldn't really see his face.

She watched as he raised the longneck in his hand and took a sip. What was he thinking, sitting out there all by himself? She longed to go and ask him.

But she didn't. She got into bed and resolutely shut her eyes.

The next morning Ethan was gone when she got up. He'd left her a note on the kitchen table saying he had a couple of meetings in town and he'd see her at the house when she got back from lunch with the girls.

She felt deflated somehow. That he was gone. That she wouldn't see him until the afternoon.

Really, she had to stop this…obsessing over him. He was finally giving her a little space and she ought to enjoy having a few hours to herself for a change.

She had her breakfast, baked a batch of double-fudge cookies and then spent the remainder of the morning at her desk, handling general correspondence for Ethan—writing letters he'd outlined for her, answering emails that didn't require his personal touch. Beyond dealing with mail and messages, she went over the reports he'd done on their work in the field the past week and a half. He'd sent them to her computer and she proofread them for errors, getting them ready to forward to Midland.

There was also an email from the broker she'd hooked up with in Midland. One of the two storefronts she had her eye on for the bakery had just taken a serious dip in asking price. The broker said the seller was really motivated now. Was Lizzie ready to make an offer?

She wrote him back that she would think it over and have an answer for him within the next couple of days.

The morning passed quickly enough. She met her new friends at the Tottering Teapot at noon. As always when she got together with Allaire and crew, she had a great time. They got after her some more about opening her bakery in Thunder Canyon. To make them stop, she promised again to think about it—and then realized that, maybe, she really *was* thinking about it.

Which totally surprised her. Sometimes a person just never knew the secrets of her own mind....

Erin said the French baker had sent her a check while she and Corey were in the Bahamas, a full refund of her money for the cake he'd failed to bake. Erin added, "He also sent a very stiffly worded apology. I felt a little sorry for the poor guy, if you want to know the truth." A glowing smile lit up her beautiful face. "But I guess I can afford to feel sorry for him because our Lizzie saved me from one of the worst tragedies any bride can face."

Our Lizzie. Okay, Lizzie really liked the sound of that.

And yes, after lunch, she did wander down the street to check out the empty bakery again. Her heart turned over when she saw the for-sale sign in the window. She realized she had been hoping it might be there.

Her hands were shaking a little as she got out her BlackBerry and entered the Realtor's name and company: Bonnie Drake, Thunder Creek Real Estate. She punched in the contact numbers from the sign.

It didn't mean she would actually call one of the numbers.

But, well, every day she stayed in Thunder Canyon, she found herself growing more attached to the place. And now, with Ethan learning to accept the changes that were coming, she could see how it could work. They could run into each other now and then, in town or at some local event, and it wouldn't have to be an awkward moment. They could simply smile and say hi.

And walk on by.

That it could actually be that way now should have cheered her.

But it didn't. It only made her sad. She really needed to snap out of this funk.

When she got back to the house, he wasn't there. He called about two to say he was over in Bozeman meeting with a couple of landmen. He'd be back late. She didn't need to have dinner ready or wait up for him.

"Tomorrow," he said before he hung up, "be ready by eight-thirty in the morning. Breakfast up at the resort."

"That's right. It's the golf-cart and horseback tour...."

"Dress for riding."

She said she would be ready. And he hung up.

And she felt…bereft. Just draggy and sad and totally neglected.

So she spent the rest of the day baking. She made bread and croissants, a chocolate peanut-butter pie and raspberry kuchen.

Baking, as always, lifted her spirits considerably. By the time she turned in that night at ten, Ethan was not yet home and she told herself she really didn't care. He had his life and she had hers and she was just fine with it being that way.

Total lie, yes. But a comforting one, nonetheless.

* * *

In the morning, he was dressed in Wranglers, a chambray shirt and rawhide boots, an old bandana tied around his neck, ready to go when she emerged from her rooms at 8:20.

"Chocolate peanut-butter pie *and* raspberry kuchen," he accused. "I came in at eleven and there they were."

She grinned. "I hope you had some of each."

"I did. Keep that up and I'll have to poke a new notch in all of my belts."

She thought how she'd love to wrap her arms around him and claim a nice, long good-morning kiss. And then she wondered if he'd been out with someone last night— someone other than a couple of landmen. Someone pretty and petite, someone with well-behaved hair who didn't dither over saying yes to what she wanted.

He was watching her kind of thoughtfully. "Something bothering you?"

"And you ask that why?"

"You baked bread. And croissants, too. And also double-fudge cookies."

"So?"

"That much baking usually means there's something you're upset about. When your dad died, I gained ten pounds, remember? Took me months of busting my ass at the gym to lose it."

I think I'm in love with you and I also think I want to buy a bakery right here in Thunder Canyon....

No. Really. Not now. It wasn't the time.

If any time ever would be. "We should get going."

He frowned, but then he agreed, "Yeah, you're right."

They took their hats and jackets from the pegs by the door to the garage and headed for the resort.

* * *

There were six of them in the group, as it turned out. Lizzie, Ethan, Grant, Connor and Tori McFarlane—and also Grant's wife, Stephanie.

Grant seemed especially pleased to have his wife with them. Steph, as everyone called her, was a Thunder Canyon native, like Grant. She ran the family ranch. They had a four-month-old, Andre John, whom they called AJ. Grant's mom was watching the baby so Steph and Grant could have a day to themselves.

They all had breakfast at the Grubstake, the resort's coffee and sandwich shop. And then they toured the golf course. That took over an hour. Like most golf courses, it was lovely and green with lots of nice trees and a few gorgeous wind-ruffled ponds. But, well, what else was there to say about it? Lizzie had never been much of a golfer.

Ethan, Grant and Connor agreed to meet the next morning at six. They would play all eighteen holes, so Ethan could get a feel for the course.

They went to the stables next, where their horses were already tacked up and waiting for them. Grant had ordered a picnic from one of the resort kitchens. He and Steph carried the food on their mounts in saddle baskets.

It was a beautiful day, the sky as blue as a baby's eyes, dotted here and there with cottony clouds. They took a series of switchbacks, moving upward, past a settlement of pricey-looking resort condos. Some of them, Grant explained, were for renting out to guests who wanted more of a private living situation than that offered in the hotel at the main clubhouse. And some of them were owned by regular resort visitors.

Farther up, spaced wide apart, were a series of one-of-a-kind cabins for big-spending guests who wanted total privacy. These Grant pointed out from the trail at a distance. Lizzie thought each cabin looked so inviting. Each was built of natural stone or logs and surrounded by tall evergreens.

They continued to wind their way up the mountain. Gradually, the trees thinned out as they reached the higher elevations. Abundant wildflowers grew on the windy, open mountainside. It was up there, not far below the rocky, snow-crested peaks, by a bright little stream, that Steph suggested they stop for lunch.

They hobbled the horses. Under a lone, wind-twisted spruce tree, they spread the big blanket Grant had brought, anchoring the corners against the gusty, cold wind with rocks they found on the hillside. They all had their jackets on by then.

But the view was so spectacular that nobody minded the cold. Spread out far below them were wild, overgrown canyons and green rolling pastureland. You could even see the town itself, looking quaint and picturesque in the distance.

They all got comfortable and shared the light meal. There were various excellent cheeses, fresh-baked bread, fruit, summer sausage and sparkling water.

Lizzie spread brie on a slice of crusty bread. "Food always tastes best when you're out in the open."

Ethan, who sat next to her, raised his bottle of sparkling water. "To good food, good company—and the great view."

They all joined in the toast.

A moment later, Ethan leaned close. "Admit it." He pitched his voice for her ears alone. "You love it here. Thunder Canyon is one of those places. You come for a visit and before you know it, you realize that you're already home."

She was all too aware of him, of the lean line of his

jaw, of the shape of his lips—lips she had kissed when she shouldn't have.

Lips she longed to kiss again.

She made herself meet his dark, knowing eyes. "Okay, I admit it. I love it here."

His smile was slow and also contagious. "I knew it," he said. And nothing more.

Lizzie spotted the deep-blue flowers growing along the stream bank as they were shaking out the blanket, getting ready to mount up again. They were low-growing flowers, maybe eight inches high, the nodding blossoms in clusters, shaped like tiny thimbles.

Steph saw her admiring them. "Mountain bluebells," she said. "They don't grow tall so high up, but they sure are pretty, aren't they?"

"Yes," Lizzie agreed. "Oh, yes, they are."

It seemed, somehow, an omen. Instead of the Texas Bluebell Bakery, why not the Mountain Bluebell?

An image took form in her mind of a nice wide wooden sign above her bakery door, a sign she would hire Allaire to paint for her. The Mountain Bluebell, it would say in proud, tall block letters, with a sprig of blue thimble-shaped flowers nodding over the words.

She turned to mount up and found Ethan, already on the bay mare he was riding, watching her. Even shadowed by the brim of his hat, it seemed to her he had the strangest expression on his handsome face.

"What?" she demanded.

He laughed. "Not a thing, Lizzie. Not a thing."

Chapter Nine

They got back to the house at six. Ethan said he was going out for dinner. She'd have the evening to herself again.

She knew then, with a grim sense of certainty, that there had to be someone else.

Someone else. How ridiculous. How could there be someone else when they'd never been together in the first place?—not in *that* way.

Not in the man-woman way.

She put on a smile. "Have a great time."

He gave her one of those long, unreadable looks he'd been giving her way too often lately. "Thanks, I will." And he went to his rooms to shower and change.

She didn't hang around waiting to watch him go. No way. She headed for her own room, where she picked up the phone to call the broker in Midland and let him know she'd changed her mind about buying a bakery in Texas.

It was a brief conversation. He spent a minute or two

trying to convince her not to be hasty. But then he seemed
to get that she'd made up her mind. He wished her luck and
told her to give him a call if there was any way he could
help her again.

After that, she looked up the Realtor's numbers she'd
taken from the for-sale sign at the empty bakery. But then
she backed out of the contact without dialing.

It didn't seem right to go ahead with her new plans until
she'd talked to Ethan about it—and no, not because she
would ever let him change her mind.

Uh-uh. She was set on her course now. She was going to
live right here in Montana. She had a whole new perspec-
tive on the situation now and she could see that she'd been
much too hung up on recreating the past. She realized that
she needed to move beyond her family's lost bakery. She
needed to create something new, something all her own.

And she was going to do exactly that.

But still, she felt that she had to share her plans with
Ethan before the fact, before she began to make them a
reality. It seemed the least she could do, to forewarn him
that she was staying in Thunder Canyon, too.

Should she tell him now?

No, not right this minute but soon. She would choose a
moment when he wasn't on his way out the door.

After he left, she made herself a sandwich for dinner
and had a big, fat slice of chocolate peanut-butter pie for
dessert. She went to her desk and paid some bills. And then
she went online to instant banking to see if her paycheck
had come through from TOI for the month.

It had. And then some.

That ginormous bonus Ethan had promised she would
get if she stuck with him until the end of July?

Already deposited.

Lizzie gaped at the entry. And then she blinked several

times in rapid succession, certain she must be having some kind of hallucination.

But no. When she looked again, that giant direct deposit was still there, way before it should have been.

And the only way that could have happened was if Ethan had put it through early.

She logged out of instant banking and shut down her computer.

And then, kind of moving on autopilot, she went to the family room, where she turned on the TV, chose a movie on Showtime and settled in to watch the whole thing. She would not be turning in. Not until after Ethan got home.

There was just no point in putting off the talk she needed to have with him. She was waiting up for him tonight and she was telling him about her change of plans when he got home. She was also asking him why he'd decided to pay her that bonus more than a month ahead of time—well, unless he brought someone home with him.

If he brought someone home with him, he would be much too busy to listen to what Lizzie had to say. Too busy up in the master suite.

With the door closed.

Oh, God. The numb, confused feeling she'd had since she'd seen the bonus in her bank account was suddenly replaced by sheer misery.

It hurt so bad to think that he might show up with some pretty little thing on his arm. More than once, she almost turned off the TV and went to bed. At least if she went to bed, she wouldn't have to see him with someone else.

But of course, she knew she was being ridiculous. If he came home with company, chances were she would see the woman eventually anyway—probably at breakfast. Now, that would be an experience. Cooking breakfast for Ethan's new girlfriend…

It was too ironic. How many breakfasts had she cooked for Ethan's various lady friends? A lot of them. Before now, she'd been happy to do it. Most of the women he dated were too skinny anyway. They could use a healthy breakfast. She'd enjoyed coddling them, making them feel comfortable. She'd known they wouldn't be around that long and, deep in her heart, she'd felt kind of sorry for each one of them.

Sorry and a little bit superior, too, a little bit smug. She'd been so sure that she would never put herself in a position to get her heart stomped on by a rich player's fancy boots.

Lizzie blew a few wild strands of hair out of her eyes and promised herself she would never feel smug about anything ever again. And as for tonight, well, she wasn't running and hiding in her room. She needed to just stick it out and wait up till he came home.

The movie ended. She started watching a second one.

And then, finally, at a little before eleven, as she dozed in the easy chair, she shook her head to wake herself up—and saw Ethan standing in the doorway to the hall.

Alone.

Or at least, there was no one tiny and adorable anywhere in sight.

His hair was windblown and he wore new jeans and dress boots, a plain dark shirt and a beautifully cut sport jacket. He gave her his trademark slow smile. "You're half-asleep." He shrugged out of the jacket, swung it behind him and let it dangle by a finger. "Why aren't you in bed?"

She blew that persistent curl of hair out of her eyes again. "I need to talk to you. Are you alone?"

"Last time I checked, yeah." He was giving her that steady look he'd given her way too often lately, that look that made her feel he could see inside her head—and maybe under her clothes, as well.

She sat up straighter, smoothed her hair, which she knew was sticking out on the sides and flattened in the back, and pressed her lips together to keep from saying too much. But then she couldn't stand it. She said it anyway. "I thought maybe you were out with, um, someone new."

Another long, unwavering look. "No, I was on my own tonight."

"Well." Relief poured through her, cool and refreshing as a mountain spring. And her heart had set up a racket inside her chest. It pounded so loud that she almost feared he might hear it—though of course she knew he couldn't. "All right, then."

He was looking down now, the jacket still dangling back over his shoulder. He seemed to be studying those fine boots of his. "Dinner was about business. I've bought a three-story brick office building over on State Street, a block from the town square. It will be my new headquarters for TOI, Montana. I made the offer yesterday while you were at lunch. And I accepted the seller's counteroffer this evening. And then, to celebrate, I had dinner with the seller. I liked him. He got caught in the crunch when the market tanked and was only too happy to give me a killer lowball price just to unload it."

A building. He'd bought a building in town. Of course. That made perfect sense.

And she realized she felt a little hurt, even though she knew she had no right to be. In the past, he would always keep her in the loop when he made a deal such as the one he'd just described. He would want to know what she thought of the purchase, and get her impressions of the various people involved. He'd always claimed he appreciated her insights.

But for some reason, he'd seen the building and then

signed the papers without letting her know what was happening.

He left the doorway and he came toward her in long, purposeful strides. Her skin kind of tingled just watching him approach. He was so glorious and manly and he looked so good in his jeans.

The TV was still on. She shook herself out of her reverie of inappropriate desire, raised the remote and pressed the power button. The flat-screen went dark as he tossed the jacket on the back of the chair beside her and then sat down.

"All right," he said. "I'm home. What did you want to talk to me about?"

Where to start? "I checked my bank balance after you left."

"Fascinating," he remarked, meaning it wasn't. He swung his boots up onto the ottoman.

"You already paid me that bonus I'm not supposed to get until the end of next month."

He shrugged, a lazy lifting of one hard shoulder. "You were going to get it anyway. Why not now rather than later?"

"Well, that wasn't the deal, though. What if I packed up tomorrow and walked out on you?"

He slanted her a look. "Like you would try and cheat me, Lizzie. Cheating's not in you. We both know that."

Okay, he was right. She would never cheat him. Still... "It's only that I have this feeling that I've taken advantage of you."

"Well, stop it. You haven't."

"Yeah, I kind of have. It was too much money in the first place, just for two extra months. I shouldn't have taken the deal. It wasn't ethical of me, but I was greedy."

He chuckled, a sound that made her body ache somehow.

With yearning. With something very close to need. "Lizzie, Lizzie, Lizzie. Don't waste your energy on guilt. There's no call for that. You were worth every penny of that bonus. Even if you got up from that chair right now, walked out of this house and never came back, I'd consider myself way ahead in any cost-benefit analysis of your term of employment, both at TOI and as my housekeeper."

She felt as if she might cry and that thoroughly annoyed her. As a rule, she wasn't the type to turn on the waterworks at the drop of a hat. But lately, her tears always seemed to be lurking way too close to the surface. She swallowed, sniffed, ordered them gone. And she said, "Well, thank you. But since we got back from eastern Montana, I've hardly done any work for you."

"I'll say it again. You haven't taken advantage of me." His voice was gruff. "Get over it." He held her gaze. His eyes were darker than ever right then, dark and endlessly deep. "If anyone's been taking advantage, it's been me. And not only with my fatheaded campaign to keep you glued to my side until you gave up your own dream to answer my phone and bake my muffins for the rest of your life."

"Oh, Ethan…"

"I've been thinking." He watched her so steadily, so seriously. "About you."

Warmth spread through her. "You have, huh?"

He gave a slow nod. "Thinking that if your goal hadn't been to own a bakery, I'd have lost you as my assistant long ago. You'd have your own office at TOI by now. You know that, don't you?"

She figured he wasn't expecting false modesty from her. "Yeah, but that wasn't what I wanted."

"So, then, let's talk about what you do want, Lizzie Landry."

You, Ethan. I want you. The words echoed in her mind. But right then, she didn't quite have the guts to say them.

And besides, there was something else she wanted, too. She wanted to realize her dream at last. And her dream was the subject at hand right now. "I've changed my mind about going back to Texas. I want to buy a bakery that's for sale on Main Street, right here in Thunder Canyon."

She waited for his shocked reaction.

It didn't come. He asked, "La Boulangerie, you mean?"

Now she was the one with her mouth hanging open. "You already knew?"

He made a low sound in the affirmative. "I had a feeling you were changing your mind about Thunder Canyon, that you were starting to really like it here."

"Oh, Ethan. I have. I do."

"I drove by that bakery on the way to sign the contract for the office building. I noticed the for-sale sign. Bonnie Drake's the Realtor."

"Yes."

"Bonnie's also *my* Realtor. So after I dealt with the papers for the office building, I asked her about the bakery. She says the owner is eager to sell. He wants to return to France, evidently."

"You think I could get a good deal, then?"

"I think you could get a terrific deal."

She let out a soft, disbelieving laugh and covered her face with her hands. "This is so not the way I expected this conversation to go."

He chuckled, too. "You expected me to be an ass?"

She lowered her hands and met his gaze. "I really didn't know how you would react."

"I told you I was through being an ass, didn't I?"

"Yes, Ethan, you did."

"You should start believing in me—at least a little." He held out his hand between their two chairs.

She took it without so much as a second's hesitation. His fingers closed around hers, strong and warm, and the now familiar thrill shivered up her arm. "I do believe in you."

He lifted her hand and he pressed his warm lips to the back of it. The touch of his mouth to her skin felt so good that she had to stifle a sharp gasp of pleasure. He lowered their joined hands but didn't let go. "I have a plan."

"Tell me."

"I'm pretty sure I can start moving into my new building in two weeks, right after Independence Day weekend."

"That's fast."

"It's empty. It should be no problem to close on the property quickly. We'll get right on the inspections, see that any necessary repairs are done. And I'm going to talk to HR down in Midland, see if there's someone clerical, someone on staff now and already trained. Someone who would be willing to relocate here temporarily, with an eye toward staying if everything works out."

"My…replacement, you mean?" Even though his finding someone new was what she wanted, it still caused a twinge of sadness to see it happening, to know that someone else was really going to take her place.

He didn't answer her question—not directly anyway. "I would want my new assistant to start on the fifth of July."

She forced a cheerfulness she didn't exactly feel. "And that way I would have almost a month to train her—or him."

"No, you're going to be much too busy for that. I'll make sure they send me someone with experience, someone who's ready to hit the ground running."

"But I don't… What do you mean, Ethan?"

"I mean, if you meet with Bonnie Drake and you can get as good a deal as I think you can, you should buy that bakery fully equipped ASAP. And I also mean that I would be letting you go early. On the fifth of July."

It wasn't right. She'd promised to stay with him until July 31. "No, that wasn't the deal."

"So what? I'm changing the terms."

"Ethan, it's not right."

"I'm the boss. If I say it's right, there's not a thing wrong with it. And if all goes according to plan, your replacement will be here and ready to take over by the fifth. And you'll have a new full-time job."

"I will?" She almost didn't dare believe what he seemed to be telling her.

But then he said it, right out loud, "You'll be running yourself ragged getting ready for your grand opening."

It was too huge. Too amazing. Too wonderful for words. Lizzie couldn't control herself. With a screech of pure joy, she leaped from her chair. "Oh, Ethan!"

Still stretched out with his feet up, he gave her the slow, lazy once-over, starting at the flip-flops on her feet and ending with her ill-behaved hair. "Whoa, Lizzie. Could you show a little enthusiasm, you think?"

"Get up here. Get up here now." She dragged on his hand until he swung his boots to the floor and rose to stand with her.

"What now?" His mouth kicked up at one corner as he arched a straight dark eyebrow.

She grabbed him by his big shoulders. "I will pay you back the bonus. It isn't fair that you should—"

He stopped her with a finger against her lips. "Shh. Listen. You're keeping that bonus."

"But it's not—"

"Lizzie."

"What?"

"Don't argue with the boss."

"Oh, Ethan."

"Enough about the bonus. Please?"

"You are the best friend I ever had and I don't know how to tell you how much I… How much it means to me. Not only that you're finally seeing what I need to do in my life, but also that you're…well, you're…" She ran out of words. Because there *were* no words.

He found them, though. "Willing to help you get what you want?"

She clapped her hands in ecstasy, gave him a double thumbs-up. "Yes. That. Exactly that."

He laughed. "You're happy. I like that."

She dropped her hands to her sides, feeling just a little bit foolish. "Yeah. But I know that sometimes I do get carried away."

"It's all right. There's nothing wrong with being happy—and showing it." For a few lovely, breathless seconds, he stared at her and she stared back at him. Finally, he said, "So…I was thinking tomorrow, as soon as I get back from playing golf with Grant and Connor, you'll call Bonnie Drake and say you'd like to see the bakery. I want to go with you, if that's all right."

"Um. Go with me?"

"Yeah—when you see the place, when you meet with Bonnie. Don't worry, I won't interfere. But it never hurts to have backup when you're making an important deal, or to have a sounding board when it gets down to negotiating."

It was so generous of him. She'd been thinking she would need to get her own Realtor for this. But Bonnie Drake had already done business with him and knew he was one of the rich Texas Traubs. If Ethan had her back, well, she felt okay about going directly through the Drake woman.

And suddenly, she just couldn't stop herself. She yanked him close and hard. "Kiss me, Ethan. Kiss me now." She didn't wait to see if he would follow her instructions. No way. She leaned in fast and she pressed her mouth to his.

He made a low noise in his throat, a growly sort of sound, a very…exciting sort of sound, actually.

And then his big arms came around her and he was holding her as hard as she held him and they were kissing and kissing.

Oh, it was wonderful. Lovely. So thrilling.

To have his arms around her again, to feel his hard chest crushing her breasts, and also, well, that other hardness, lower down, the one that proved he really did like her—and not just as a friend.

It was wonderful, fabulous, to kiss him and kiss him some more, with his breath so warm in her mouth and their tongues all tangled up together.

At last! she was thinking. She really didn't care what the future might bring right then. She wanted Ethan. She wanted him *now*.

But then he took her face in his two hands and broke the magical, beautiful kiss. "Lizzie…" He sounded almost regretful.

Huh? What was there to regret? Everything was going along just fine as far as she was concerned. With a groan, she leaned in and tried to capture his lips again.

He didn't let her. "Lizzie." He said her name more insistently that time.

With another groan, a frustrated one, she opened her eyes. "Oh, Ethan. What?"

He looked at her so intently, his dark eyes soft and tender. And she did love it when his lips were red from kissing her. It made her feel limp and yearning and lovely inside.

But then he spoke. "I don't think we should rush into anything, you know?"

Her desire-fogged mind strove to register the words—and the meaning behind them. "But I don't get it. I thought you *wanted*…" Ugh. How to go on from there? Why should she even try?

Suddenly, she was feeling much less than limp and yearning. She was starting to feel just slightly rejected.

He spoke gently. "Lizzie…"

"You keep saying my name. It's not reassuring." She took his wrists, guided them away from her and stepped back. "Sorry. I got a little carried away, I guess." All at once, it was hard to look at him. So she didn't. She stared down at her flip-flops.

"Come on, Lizzie."

He was being sweet and considerate and she knew that. In fact, he'd been absolutely terrific to her tonight, telling her he was letting her go early, offering to help her get the property she wanted.

She needed to get a grip on herself, to stop acting like a rejected lover. Even if that was exactly how she felt. She lifted her chin and fluffed at her hair. "Don't tell me. It's my hair. Or maybe these ancient sweats, huh? I'm not exactly dressed for seduction."

A grin tried to pull at the side of his mouth. "Your hair is adorable. I love those sweats."

"Hah. Nothing about me is adorable. I'm more the… sturdy type. The kind of woman you can count on."

"Yes, you are. But you're also adorable."

She couldn't resist asking, "So how come you don't drag me up to your room and have your way with me?" He opened his mouth to answer and then apparently changed his mind. "What?" she demanded. "Say it. Please."

He shook his head. "You should be sure, that's all."

"How much more sure can a woman get? I just threw myself at you, in case you didn't notice."

"Oh, I noticed."

"Well, then?"

"It doesn't seem right."

She couldn't help it. She rolled her eyes. "Honestly. *Right?* Now you're worrying about whether it seems right? For over two weeks now, you've made it more than clear that all I have to do is say the word. So finally, I did, I said the word. And all of a sudden, you're into the ethics of the whole thing."

"I've been thinking, that's all."

"Yeah, got that. You've been thinking way too much, if you ask me."

"You're my assistant. How tacky is that, to be sleeping with my assistant? How…predictable, you know?"

She couldn't help it. She laughed. "You won't make love with me because it would be predictable?"

"Don't make fun of me. Please. I'm trying to do the right thing here, in case you didn't notice."

"Well, you're kind of oversharing."

Now he looked glum. "I am?"

"Yeah, a little. And think of it this way, if everything goes according to plan, I won't be your assistant for all that much longer. So maybe this thing with us isn't as tacky and predictable as you seem to think."

"It's not only that."

"Oh, great." She blew hair out of her eyes again. "How did I know there was more?"

"We don't want the same things, Lizzie. I'm not…your kind of guy. We both agree that I'm not."

"So? That didn't seem to bother you before."

"Like I said, I've been thinking. About the consequences of my possible actions."

"Well, that's new and different."

"Could you just not insult me? Please."

"Sorry. Really. Go on."

"You're important to me, Lizzie. I don't want to lose you, you know? And when it ends…"

Okay, that hurt. "*When,* huh? Not *if?* Couldn't there be just a little bit of *if* in this whole situation?"

"Lizzie, I'm thirty-seven years old. I've never once even considered getting married. My relationships with women have the shelf life of an avocado with the skin peeled off."

She hated to hear him say that, mostly because it was true. "But…what if you wanted to change?"

"We've been through this. You know that I really like my life the way it is. There have to be statistics out there on guys like me, statistics that say a woman is more likely to get hit by a runaway train than to make a lasting relationship with someone like me."

She could really start to get annoyed with him about now. "I think you have a few more years before you become a statistic. Give yourself a little credit, will you?"

"I'm just trying to be realistic, that's all. And come on, don't look at me like that."

"I can't help it. You make it all sound so hopeless."

His expression remained painfully somber. "Not hopeless. Just not especially promising."

She hated that he was right. And she did give him credit for holding back, for trying *not* to get something started between them that could ruin their friendship—especially now that they knew they were going to be living in the same small town. He had a point, he truly did. She should be considering how important their friendship was, too.

She gave it up. "You're right. We don't need to go rushing into anything." She reached out and clasped his shoulder, the gesture of a friend. And she studiously ignored the little thrill she got just from putting her hand on him. Because she *was* his friend. And she intended to stay his friend. No matter what. "Thanks in great part to you, I have a big day tomorrow."

He made a low noise in his throat. "Yeah, you do."

"I want to be at the top of my game for it."

And finally, he smiled. "I hear you."

"So I think I'll go to bed now. Alone."

"Good idea." He reached out then, wrapped his big hand gently around the back of her neck and pulled her in close. "Good night, Lizzie." He pressed his warm lips to her forehead.

It felt so good, his hand against her nape, his lips on her skin, the warmth of his fine body so close. She really, really wanted to tip her chin up just enough that his mouth could meet hers.

But no.

They were friends. They weren't rushing into anything. And she had a big day tomorrow.

She stepped back. He let her go. It caused a small ache within her, to lose the press of his lips on her flesh, the lovely clasp of his hand on her nape. "Good night, Ethan."

And she turned and left him there.

Chapter Ten

Ethan watched her go, a tall, no-nonsense woman in baggy gray sweats. Her hair was kind of mashed in the back.

He'd never seen anyone so beautiful—going or coming.

He wanted…everything for her. The rich, full life she deserved. In this great little town where she already had about a hundred friends. Now he'd finally realized that he couldn't bear to hold her back, he wanted her to have the bakery of her dreams.

Not only *wanted,* but he was also going to make it happen.

He went over to the wet bar, put some crushed ice in a glass and added two fingers of good scotch. He sipped the drink slowly, feeling pretty good about himself in spite of the ache in his jeans.

Sometimes a guy just did what was right for a really good person. Sometimes a guy chose a great friendship over a hot roll in the sack because there were other things in life that mattered more than sex.

Yeah, there were times when he got a little hazy on that, on what could matter more than sex. But not now, not when it came to Lizzie.

Tomorrow, if no unforeseen issues cropped up, she would buy herself a bakery. And after that, he'd get two last weeks with her—well, twelve days, to be exact. Until the fifth of July.

And when she was no longer working for him, they could still keep their friendship. Because he wasn't going to mess up what he had with her.

He was going to keep his hands off her. Just enjoy her company. And leave it at that.

When Ethan returned from the resort at ten the next morning, Lizzie was sitting at the kitchen table wearing a slim tan skirt and a silk shirt the exact color of her gray-green eyes. Her hair was smooth, tamed-looking. Her makeup was light as always. A little bit of shadow to bring out her eyes, and gloss on her lips that made them look wet.

Wet and much too kissable.

Forget the kissable, he commanded himself. He wasn't going to be thinking about kissing her. He wasn't going to imagine messing up her hair so it got wild the way he liked it best, or think about slowly unbuttoning that silvery-green shirt, spreading it open, unclasping her bra and seeing her breasts for the very first time.

Uh-uh.

That wasn't what they were about, him and Lizzie.

She had a glowing, self-satisfied smile on her face. "So how was the golfing?"

"It's a great course. The fairways are tight."

"Uh. Good to know."

"Spoken like a woman who knows zip about golf. And let me guess, you already called Bonnie."

Her smile widened. "I did. She says she can meet us there at eleven."

"Well, all right."

"Did you get breakfast?"

"Yeah, at the Grubstake. I'll just jump in the shower and be ready in plenty of time."

Everything went as Ethan intended it to.

They met the Realtor in front of the bakery and she let them in. It was an attractive little shop, with high, pressed-tin ceilings and wide plank floors. In the front area, Lizzie spent a lot of time behind the counter, checking out the display cases, the cold cases, the bread slicer, the cash register, the vintage Italian espresso machine.

In the back, she had to open every door and get a close look at each piece of equipment. That took over an hour, after which they went down the hallway to the back exit, pausing to have a look inside both of the restrooms, and then going on outside to see the good-size parking lot that the bakery shared with the gift shop next door.

There was extra storage upstairs, as well as a two-bedroom shotgun-style apartment. The living room of the apartment was in the front, overlooking Main Street, and was roomy and bright with the same wide plank floors as in the shop below. Lizzie seemed charmed by the farm-style sink in the kitchen and the checkerboard linoleum on the kitchen floor. The one bath had an old claw-foot tub with a shower attachment added on.

Throughout the tour of the property, Ethan hung back as he'd told her he would. It was Lizzie's deal, after all. He was only there to make certain she got what she wanted at a reasonable price. As he watched her turning on faucets, peering into closets and cabinets and even the oven, he tried to picture her living there.

The kitchen was really small, more of a hallway than a room, nothing like the expansive, state-of-the-art kitchens she'd run living with him. How could she be satisfied with such a dinky little space to do her cooking and endless baking in?

But then he had to admit that he was only being negative. She would have the whole bakery downstairs in which to practice her love of cooking. She probably wouldn't need any more of a kitchen in her living space than the apartment provided.

The bedrooms were not especially exciting. One was in the center of the space, with a single window that gave a view of the brick wall next door. But the larger one, in the back, had two windows overlooking the parking lot and a nice view of State Street and beyond.

Bonnie Drake said the French baker, Aubert Pelletier, was willing to sell everything in the place. Lizzie told the Realtor she'd keep that in mind.

Once the tour was finally finished, Bonnie had to rush off to another appointment, but she said she'd be free that afternoon in case Lizzie had more questions for her. Ethan and Lizzie went to lunch at the Hitching Post. He watched her across the table. Her cheeks were pink and her eyes had a definite gleam in them.

"Well?" he asked, once the waitress had served them their burgers.

"I want it." She popped a French fry into her mouth. "I'm buying that bakery."

He laughed. "I kind of had a feeling you were."

They discussed what she should offer and the state of the equipment, which Lizzie said was excellent. "One thing that baker knew, it was equipment. All the best brands and all of it in great condition."

"So you think you're ready to make your offer?"

"Oh, yes, I do."

So at four that afternoon, in Bonnie's office at Thunder Creek Real Estate, Lizzie submitted her offer on Aubert Pelletier's bakery. She would put down a significant amount in cash and she had a letter from a local banker acquired an hour earlier with Ethan's help that guaranteed her a loan for the balance.

Lizzie wanted to take possession on the fifth of July, when she would move into the apartment upstairs and start working furiously toward the day when the Mountain Bluebell Bakery opened for business.

Aubert Pelletier, who was currently staying in New York, would have forty-eight hours to take the offer or to counter. Bonnie assured Lizzie that she was in close contact with the bakery's owner and that Pelletier was eager to settle all his business in the United States and be on his way back home.

When they left Bonnie's office, Ethan suggested they go out to celebrate.

"Uh-uh," said Lizzie. "Not until the deal is done."

"What? You're afraid you might jinx it by celebrating too early?"

She laughed and put her hand against his mouth. "Shh. Don't even say that word."

Her fingers were so cool and soft. He wanted to kiss them, but he didn't. He gently pushed her hand away and teased, "Celebrate? I shouldn't say *celebrate?*"

"Ha-ha." She wrinkled her nose at him. "I want to go home, if you don't mind."

Home. He found himself thinking that in no time at all, she'd be calling that dinky apartment over the bakery her home. He didn't like that much, but he knew he had to get used to it. Lizzie was moving on and his job as her friend was to support her in that.

She added, "I'd like a nice, quiet evening to…come to grips with the huge step I just took."

He knew what she was really saying. "You want to cook. It will relax you."

Her eyes shone, green as spring grass. "You know me so well."

He ached to reach for her, to pull her close, to kiss her, right there on Cedar Street, and not care that anyone driving by might see.

But he didn't. He remembered the objective: to do what was best for Lizzie.

And kissing her was not it.

They went back to the house. Lizzie made lasagna and garlic bread and a fresh green salad. He opened a bottle of Chianti and they toasted to change and a bright, exciting future for each of them.

When dinner was over, he helped her clear the table and then he went to his office to take care of some paperwork. When he came out at ten, the house was quiet, the kitchen dark.

He drank a glass of water from the tap and stood at the counter, staring into the dimness, thinking that it was going to be very strange to live in a house without Lizzie. He wasn't really looking forward to that.

But he would manage. Eventually, he would get used to the new order of things. He would adjust.

"Come with me to the resort this afternoon."

Lizzie glanced up from her computer at her desk off the kitchen. It was a little after eleven Thursday morning. "Yes. Anything to take my mind off watching the clock, waiting for the phone to ring with Aubert Pelletier's response to my offer…."

"Stop worrying," Ethan said.

"I'm trying, I'm trying."

"We'll leave after lunch. Grant's arranged to have horses waiting for us. I want to take a look at the interior of a few of the condos, just to see the quality of the furnishings, the finishes, that kind of thing. And we'll get a closer look than we did Tuesday at a couple of those cabins higher up, too."

"Will Steph and Tori be coming?"

"Nope. Connor and Tori are out of town until tomorrow. Stephanie's busy at the Clifton ranch. Grant's got meetings. He's going to leave the keys with the stable hand. It will be just the two of us this time."

Just the two of us. It sounded downright romantic. She wished. "Want to go before lunch? I can pack some sandwiches."

"That would work."

She shut down her computer. "Give me twenty minutes, I'll be ready and so will the food."

The horses were waiting at the resort stables as promised. The groom gave them a set of keys and a map of the resort, with the route to the condos and the various cabins marked in red. Because it was the same way they'd gone Tuesday, they probably would have had no trouble finding what they were looking for. Ethan took the map anyway and thanked the groom.

They mounted and set out on the road to the condos, side by side. It was another gorgeous day, warm with a nice breeze. Lizzie was glad to be out in the open, glad to be with Ethan.

He sent her a smile from under the shadow of his hat.

Her heart warmed. If she couldn't have it all with him, well, at least he was her friend. The best friend any girl could ever have.

They reached the condos within half an hour and toured two of them, one in the first block of buildings on the ground floor and one deeper into the complex, upstairs.

Ethan seemed pleased with the furnishings, which were all of good quality, in rich jewel colors—vivid reds, deep blues, golds and emerald greens. The small kitchens had granite counters and stainless-steel appliances. Everything was clean and well maintained.

When they left the second condo, they stood on the landing and stared out at the pine-covered mountains all around. "No surprises here," he said.

She nodded. "Just like the rest of the resort. Everything in great condition."

"Grant runs a tight operation all right." He sent her a glance. "And this is probably an unnecessary trip."

She put a finger to her lips. "Shh. Don't say that. It's a gorgeous day and the view is spectacular."

His gaze was warm. Appreciative. She basked in it.

They mounted their horses again and proceeded up the mountain.

"You hungry?" Ethan asked before they reached any of the cabins. He gestured at the open meadows that surrounded them on either side. A stand of cottonwoods at the edge of the meadow directly west of them seemed to indicate a stream nearby. "Great place for a picnic."

They rode out among the tall grasses and wildflowers, and heard the soft rushing sound of the stream as they approached it. Lizzie had brought a blanket, which they spread under a cottonwood tree right at the spot where the bank sloped away toward the creek. She had roast-beef sandwiches, bags of chips, some ripe red apples and a big thermos of iced tea.

She sat close to him on the blanket, munching an apple and indulging herself in a little fantasy of what it might be like if they were lovers. They would share a few kisses certainly, maybe take off their boots and wade in the cool, clear water of the little creek.

They might even go farther. She hadn't seen any other people since they left the settlement of condos. What would it be like to make love here, in the shade of the cottonwood trees on this breezy, sunny day?

It seemed kind of depressing that she would never know.

She glanced his way and found him watching her and she had a feeling that he was thinking more or less what she was thinking.

But she didn't ask him. Because he seemed so determined to be her friend and only her friend, it was probably better not to know.

"Nice here," she said, keeping it neutral. Safe.

He made a low noise of agreement. "Ready to move on?"

She wrapped up the remains of their meal and packed it in her saddlebag as he rolled the blanket. In no time, they were back on the horses and setting off across the meadow toward the road.

It was a little after two when they reached the first cabin. Ethan had a key to that one, so they rode right up to the front porch, tied the horses on the rail there and went in.

The door opened on a great room with a soaring two-story ceiling furnished in a comfortable rustic style. There were lots of windows letting in the daylight, framing a view of a wide deck and the piney mountains all around. The open kitchen had all the modern conveniences.

"It's beautiful," Lizzie said, as they entered the master suite which shared the deck with the great room and also had the same spectacular views.

Ethan went into the master bath, but Lizzie continued on toward the French doors that opened onto the deck. She flipped the lock and pulled the door wide and went out to stand at the railing and gaze over the canyon that fell away below.

The wind had picked up in the past half hour or so. As she stared out over the crown of trees below, she caught a faint whiff of smoke. She scanned the surrounding hillside for a sign of the source.

There was nothing.

Ethan came out through the open door. "Do you smell smoke?"

Just as he asked the question, she heard the strangest whooshing sound.

And suddenly, the hillside about a hundred yards below her was on fire.

Lizzie gasped. "Oh, my God!" She knew such things could happen, a fire smoldering in the underbrush and then, in an instant, leaping upward into the crowns of the trees.

Still, she had trouble believing her own eyes. She stared at the bright, roiling balls of vivid flame. And as she watched, with another sizzling *whoosh,* the balls of fire leaped closer, setting the tops of more trees ablaze.

It was climbing the hillside, coming straight for the cabin.

Ethan grabbed her hand, his warm fingers closing over her suddenly numb ones. "Time to go, Lizzie."

It just didn't seem real. She hung back as he tugged on her arm. "We should…call someone, shouldn't we?"

"Come on." He pulled her inside and went straight to

the phone on the nightstand. "Deader than a hammer." He slammed it back into the cradle. "They must turn it off when there's no one using the place."

"Oh, Ethan…" Now, out through the French doors, she could see the billows of smoke rising from below the deck.

"We can try a cell. As soon as we're out of here." He grabbed her hand again and they made for the front door.

Outside, the horses were snorting, tugging at their leads, agitated by the smell of smoke, which was much stronger now than it had been only moments before out on the deck. Her gray gelding shook his mane and pawed the ground.

"Easy, now, easy…" Lizzie tried to soothe him.

Ethan was already mounted. "Lizzie, need help?"

"He's a little freaked out, but I think I'm okay." She got her boot up into the stirrup and her other leg over, finding her seat. Then she bent forward and whispered more reassurances to the agitated gray. He pranced and tossed his head some more, but then seemed to settle a little.

"Fire moves toward the oxygen," Ethan said.

She patted the gray's powerful neck. "Uphill. And the wind's going that way, too."

"I'm hoping it's just in that area down the canyon and the road is safe—as of now, anyway."

She knew what he was saying. The fire would be spreading, moving up toward the road at the same time as it burned toward the cabin.

He urged his horse in the direction of the road. She guided the gray along behind him. He was already getting out his cell. "No signal," he told her. "We can try again in a few minutes, farther on. Up here, the signals seem to fade in and out."

The air swiftly thickened with acrid, throat-scratching smoke as they rode down the winding dirt driveway that led to the main road.

They reached the road within minutes and started down the mountain.

Ethan took out his phone again. "I've got a couple of bars and the resort on autodial. I'll try 911 first." He did. And shook his head. "Nothing. I'll call the resort."

That time, when he put the phone to his ear, he gave Lizzie a nod; he'd gotten through. "This is Ethan Traub," he said. And he repeated his cell number and gave their location. "There's a fire burning fast up the mountain from the canyon right below the first cabin. Call for help, please. And tell Grant Clifton… Hello? Hello?" He pulled the phone away from his ear. "That was the switchboard. I lost her."

"You think she understood?"

"I sure hope so." He put the phone away and coughed against the smoke that now filled the air. "Protect your face." He pulled up the bandana he always wore when he rode, covering his mouth and nose.

She did the same. The cloth barrier helped a little against the choking burn of the smoke.

He gave her a nod from behind his makeshift mask. "Let's get a move on."

They started down the road. The horses chuffed and snorted against the smoke. But so far, they were doing all right. If it got too much thicker, though, they would need to dismount and lead them. It looked clear ahead—lots of smoke rolling up from the canyon, but no flames so far—and Lizzie began to feel more confident that they would make it down the mountain safely.

But then, right ahead of them, a wild-eyed doe burst from the brush, up from canyon, fleeing the fire.

The terrified animal zipped across the dirt road and scrambled up the bank on the other side, spooking the already uneasy horses.

She heard Ethan talking to his mount. "Whoa, whoa, girl. Settle now, settle…" She glanced over and saw that his horse was dancing in circles.

And then her gray reared up on his hind legs. She should have been ready for that, but she wasn't. One moment she was on the back of the gray.

The next, she was flying through the air.

"Lizzie!" Ethan's voice. Calling her name.

And then she hit the ground. Hard.

The breath fled her lungs. Her teeth clanged together hard enough that she wondered if she'd cracked a few of them. She heard the furious pounding of hooves somewhere, moving away. Her horse, maybe running off?

The world had started spinning. Faster and faster. And then slowly, it resolved into a tiny pinpoint of too-bright light.

The light didn't last long. Within a second or two, everything went black.

Chapter Eleven

"Lizzie. My God. Lizzie…"

She opened her eyes. Ethan loomed above her. He looked like a bandit with the bandana still covering the lower half of his face—an absolutely terrified bandit. She realized she'd never seen him scared before. Not like he was now. Not stark-eyed, life-and-death scared.

"Hey." She blinked. Twice. Her own bandana had slipped down around her neck again. Her head hurt. And so did her teeth. But she knew where she was—flat on the ground in the middle of a dirt road. She knew what had happened. And she could still smell smoke. That smell was getting stronger. "So I'm thinking I'm not dead, after all. Tell me I'm right."

"Don't move." He slid something under her head—his jacket. "Just stay right where you are."

"Ethan, I'm fine. My horse?"

"Bolted." He yanked his own bandana down. And she

saw his lips were white with fear. For her. "Don't worry about the damn horse."

She reached up, touched his dear, frightened face. So warm. So real. "I'm okay. I really am. Please believe me. We need to get out of here."

He laid a tender hand on her forehead, stroked her hair back out of her eyes, his touch so light, so full of care. "You hit your head. Oh, God, Lizzie. You were knocked out. You could have been—"

"I said I'm fine. Let me up."

He scowled and put a hand on her shoulder, holding her down. "Lizzie—"

"I mean it. Let me up."

Reluctantly, he released her. She popped to a sitting position, groaning a little, reaching around to probe at the back of her head where there was already one heck of a goose egg taking shape. "Ugh."

He was still scowling. "I don't think you should be sitting up."

"As if we have any choice in the matter. I think we really have to get moving." She brought her hand around to the front. There was blood on her fingers. "Yuck. I'm bleeding."

Ethan swore. "Let me see."

She turned around so he could have a look. "Where's my hat?" As she asked the question, she saw it a few feet away, trampled on the road. Ethan's mare was there, too, patiently waiting beside the crumpled hat. "At least we still have a horse."

"The bleeding's not too bad," he said. "But you've got one hell of a bump back here."

"Ouch." She put her hand to her mouth and coughed against the black roiling smoke rising up from the bushes on the side of the road where the bank dropped off sharply into the canyon below. "We have to go. Quit poking at it. Help me up."

"Lizzie—"

"I can't sit here in the road all day, not with the smoke getting thicker and the fire coming closer." She pulled up her bandana to cover her nose again and held out her hand to him. "Help me up." He swore some more, but then pulled up his own bandana and gave her his hand. With his strong arm to aid her, she rose unsteadily to her feet.

As soon as she staggered upright, he got hold of her by the shoulders. "Are you dizzy?" He peered hard into her eyes.

"No, I'm not dizzy." Yes, her head hurt, but it could have been worse. "I'm fine. I mean it. My hat?"

"I'll get it." Slowly, as if he feared she might suddenly drop in a dead faint, he released her and bent to grab the hat. She brushed the dust off her jeans and shirt as best she could. "Here you go." He handed it over, bending to retrieve his balled-up, slightly bloodied jacket.

She fisted the hat back into reasonable shape and put it on. "Let's get out of here." She could see the fire now, not ten feet away, eating into the brush at the cliff edge of the road, spreading out to either side in shining red trails, the black smoke billowing, blown right at them by the wind that seemed to gust harder every second. That fire was much too close. Even Ethan's patient mare was starting to snort and circle.

He mounted up. The mare snorted once more, but seemed to calm as soon as her rider had the reins. He held down his hand and Lizzie swung up behind him.

Whoosh.

Ten yards ahead of them, right before the road turned, the fire jumped to the other side. The bushes on the upper bank burst into flame and the fire licked higher, moving on up the mountain.

Lizzie wrapped her arms around Ethan's waist and buried her face against his broad back. "Let's go—now!"

He urged the horse forward at a walk. It wasn't safe in a danger zone to go above a trot. Ethan played it extra cautious and kept the speed way down. Lizzie held on and formed a silent prayer, that they would make it, get through the fire to safety.

If anyone could get them out of there, Ethan could. She so admired him during that deadly ride. It took nerves of steel to keep the mare going slow and steady in spite of the choking smoke, the constantly increasing heat and the crackling, hissing sounds the fire made.

As if it were a living thing, and hungry, ready to jump at them and eat them alive.

In minutes, they were in the hottest area, with fire surrounding them, on either side of the road. It was like riding through a tunnel in hell.

Ethan kept the horse going steadily forward. She was a champion, that mare. She startled twice, when a jackrabbit ran directly across their path and then when drifting embers from the fire burned her sleek red-brown coat. Ethan managed to calm the horse both times, and he brushed away the burning ash with his hand.

Lizzie had the easy job. She only had to hold on and not lose her seat.

It didn't take all that long. It only seemed like forever and a day. Within maybe ten minutes of mounting behind Ethan, the smoke was thinning and the fire was mostly above and behind them. A few embers still smoldered on the canyon side of the road.

Ethan urged the mare to a trot then. "Hold on, Lizzie."

"I am. Don't worry about me."

They rode on at a brisk pace for fifteen or twenty minutes. By then, the danger was well behind them. Ethan slowed the horse and then reined her to a stop.

As he got out his phone and tried the resort again, Lizzie dared to look back the way they had come. It wasn't pretty. Thick, black smoke billowed up to the clear, blue sky. Someone surely must have seen it and turned in an alarm by now.

Ethan got through. "This is Ethan Traub— Yes? Okay. Great. Good. We made it, yeah. We're below the fire now, out of danger, on our way to the clubhouse." He ended the call and told Lizzie, "That first switchboard operator was on the ball. She called it in. The forest service is sending up crews."

As he said the words, she heard the planes overhead on their way to dump loads of fire retardant on the blaze.

Ethan clucked his tongue at the mare and she ambled on down the road again.

Lizzie's gray had made it back to the stables ahead of them. He was lathered and winded, but otherwise okay.

Ethan refused to go back to town until she'd visited the infirmary at the resort's clubhouse. The doctor checked out the bump on her head, cleaned it with disinfectant and told her he thought she would be stiff and achy tomorrow but otherwise okay. Just to be on the safe side, he ran down the danger signs to watch for with a head injury. Ethan listened with fierce concentration and promised he'd be keeping his eye on her for any sign of disorientation or sudden confusion.

Grant found them in the infirmary. He reported that the forest service already had the fire under control, thanks to Ethan's early call. The cabin was a burned-out shell, but other than that, the only damage was the torched hillside.

Ethan asked, "Do they know yet what started it?"

Grant grunted in disgust. "A couple of hikers decided to build a fire. The wind came up and the fire got away from them."

Lizzie hoped they'd escaped with their lives. "Are they okay?"

"They're fine—except for the whopping fines they'll be expected to pay. Insurance will cover our losses. But those hikers may be in for another shock if the insurance company decides to sue."

"I don't feel a hell of a lot of sympathy for them," Ethan said darkly.

"I'm just glad you two are okay," Grant told them. He asked Lizzie, "How's your head?"

"I'm fine. Really. Don't worry about me."

"She keeps saying that." Ethan reached out and put his arm around her. The last time he'd done that in front of Grant, she'd thoroughly disapproved and told Ethan so in no uncertain terms.

But now, well, everything was different.

She leaned in closer to his strength and his warmth and she sent him her most grateful smile. "I'm lucky. You saved me."

"Hardly."

She elbowed him in the ribs. "You did. You know you did. And can we please go home now?"

He was looking in her eyes and for a moment, she thought he might kiss her—right there in the infirmary, in front of the doctor and Grant Clifton.

But then he only said softy, "Sure, Lizzie. Whatever you want."

"A bath," she said, when he pulled the SUV into the garage and the big door rumbled down behind them. "I want a hot bath and I want to soak for about a year. And after that, I want reheated lasagna."

"You got it," Ethan said gruffly. And then he reached across the console and put his hand against her cheek. He seemed, since they'd made it through the fire, to need the reassurance of touching her. She completely understood. His touch made her feel better, too. He asked, "How's your head?"

"Dusty and sore like the rest of me." She gave him what she hoped was a stern look. "And stop worrying about me."

Reluctantly, he dropped his hand away.

They went inside, hung their hats and jackets back on the pegs by the door.

He asked, "You need anything?" as she was turning to go to her rooms.

She winced as she put her hand at the small of her back where she was reasonably certain a big bruise was forming. "I'll keep you posted."

He hovered close. "I'm kind of afraid to let you go off by yourself. What if you pass out or something?"

It seemed as good an excuse as any to put her hand on him. So she did. She pressed her palm to his cheek, which was getting a little sandpapery with his afternoon beard. "I am not going to pass out. I am not dizzy, nor am I confused. Or disoriented. I have none of the symptoms that might indicate approaching unconsciousness or incipient brain damage. So can we just give that a rest now, you think?"

He grumbled, "Yes, ma'am." And then he added, "But leave the door open—to the bathroom *and* the bedroom, will you? I'll be in the kitchen. And I'll be able to hear you if you scream."

She couldn't stop herself. She kissed him.

It wasn't a big deal of a kiss. On the contrary, it was no

more than a slight brush of her mouth against his. "Ethan." She breathed his name against his lips.

"What?" He tried to look disapproving. But she thought he mostly just looked so handsome and worried about her and very, very dear.

"If I'm going to pass out in the bathtub, it's unlikely I would scream first."

"Right. Exactly. All the more reason you shouldn't be taking a bath right now anyway."

She frowned at him, but in a good-natured way. "I'm taking a bath. Get used to it."

"Can you do me one favor?"

"Depends. What?"

"Give me ten minutes. I'll grab a quick shower. Then I'll sit in the kitchen and be ready in case you need me."

She shook her head. "Apparently, there is no getting through to you." She took him by those muscular shoulders and turned him around. "Go. Have your shower. Ten minutes. That's all you get."

For once, he didn't argue. He headed for the front foyer and the stairs.

She went to the kitchen, drank a tall glass of iced water and checked her email.

He was back in eight minutes flat, his lean cheeks stubble-free, smelling of soap and aftershave. It was a big improvement over the acrid scent of smoke. "All right," he growled at her. "Your turn. And don't you dare pass out and drown."

She rose from her computer and headed for her rooms before he had a chance to come up with any more objections.

As the tub filled, she got undressed and studied the damage to her poor body in the full-length mirror on the bathroom door. She did have a big bruise on her lower back as well as a few cuts and scrapes, and more bruises on her legs and arms.

But in a week or two, she would be good as new. She wasn't complaining. She'd been bucked off her horse and knocked unconscious. And then she'd ridden through a tunnel of fire. Considering the circumstances, she was in pretty good condition.

She sank into the warm, scented water with a happy sigh and for a while she just drifted, resting her head on a towel, letting the water soak the aches and pains away, smiling happily to herself. And thinking about Ethan.

Ethan. Waiting in the kitchen, worried to distraction that she might not be all right.

Ethan. The best friend she'd ever had.

Ethan. Who had saved her.

And whom she loved.

It all seemed so simple and straightforward really. She wanted Ethan.

And he was trying so hard to do the right thing. But he wanted her, too.

They had eleven days left together in this house. Eleven days they could spend denying the power of this amazing, who-knew-this-could-happen attraction between them.

Or eleven days where they could have it all.

It didn't seem such a difficult choice when she looked at it that way.

He might think otherwise. He was trying to do right by her after all. But she had a pretty strong feeling she could bring him around to her point of view.

Still smiling, she sat up and reached for the shampoo.

Ethan was getting a little bit worried.

Lizzie had disappeared into her rooms over an hour ago. He'd already been down that hallway twice, just to make certain that the door was still open, so if she did happen to call for him he would have a chance of hearing her. Both times, he'd caught the faint scent of vanilla and a hint of moisture in the air that seemed to indicate she was doing exactly what she'd told him she would be doing: taking a long, hot bath.

Both times, he'd almost spoken up, demanded a response from her, just to be certain that she was okay. But then he'd chickened out at the last minute. She'd had a rough time of it up on the mountain. It seemed only fair to let her have her damn bath in peace.

Come on, Lizzie. You're freaking me out here....

He kept picturing her lying at the bottom of the bathtub, staring up through vanilla-scented bathwater with sightless eyes. It was creepy and scary and she'd damn well better get out here within the next five minutes, or he was getting up and marching into the hallway and yelling at her to speak up and let him know that she was all right.

"Ethan." Lizzie's voice.

He swiveled his head around and saw her standing in the kitchen doorway. Her skin was all pink and soft-looking. She had a bruise on her right shoulder, two on her left forearm and one on her long, rather muscular left thigh. Her hair was shining, falling to her shoulders and drooping over her eyes, loose and wild. Just the way he liked it.

She wore a bath towel. And apparently nothing else.

Chapter Twelve

"Not fair," Ethan said in a voice that was more an animal growl than any noise a man might make. "Go put some clothes on."

She did the opposite of what he told her to do, which really didn't surprise him because she generally did everything *but* what he told her to do. She left the doorway and came toward him, her bare feet making no sound on the limestone tile of the kitchen floor.

He stood up and faced her. Which was probably a mistake, given that his physical reaction to her standing there in that towel had been instantaneous. Now it was obvious—to him, and to her.

She looked down at the ridge in his jeans and then, with a slow smile, back up into his eyes. And she kept coming. Until she was standing right in front of him and he could smell her—vanilla and a hint of something tart. Lemons, maybe—no. Oranges. Ripe, juicy oranges.

"Lizzie, come on." He groaned. He couldn't help it. "Don't do this to me."

She didn't say anything. Only lifted a hand and laid it on his chest. His heart pounded like wild horses set loose on a midnight run. He knew she could feel the pounding.

"Lizzie, don't..." That was as far as he got.

Because she slid that hand up over his shoulder and clasped the back of his neck. The towel dropped into a puddle at her feet.

He couldn't help it, couldn't stop himself. He looked down.

Into heaven.

He saw her pretty breasts with their hard pink nipples. He saw all of her, all of that soft, firm, smooth flesh. And then she did worse.

She pressed herself against him—those warm, amazing curves of hers, touching him all along the front of him. The hardness in his pants got harder.

It hurt to want her that much.

And then she leaned that fraction closer. She kissed him, her soft mouth opening beneath his.

What did she expect? A man could only go so far in trying to do the right thing. After a point, the woman he wanted and was trying desperately to protect from his bad self had to meet him halfway.

Lizzie wasn't helping him. Lizzie refused to meet him halfway.

Lizzie was blatantly, shamelessly leading him into temptation.

And temptation was just too fine of a place to be.

He gave in.

With a low, angry, frustrated growl, he reached out and hauled her hard against him.

Heaven. Oh, yeah. Lizzie, naked, in his arms. He ran

his hungry hands across the silky skin of her long, strong back. He cupped the sweet twin curves of her bottom in his palms.

She gave a little moan into his mouth. He drank that sound. It tasted of her eagerness, of her warmth and her breath. Her sounds were his—*she* was his. Her body, her mouth, that annoying, too-quick brain of hers, her big heart, her goodness. All the things that were Lizzie.

For now, at least, they were his. *She* was his.

A bed, he thought. *We really need a bed.*

Hers was closest. So, still kissing her, still holding on tight, he bent enough to get one arm under her knees. The other, he used to hold her shoulders.

He straightened, lifting her high in his arms. She let out a strangled little squeak of surprise. He smiled against her parted lips.

And then, with a happy little sigh, she wrapped her arms around his neck and went on kissing him. She was no lightweight, his Lizzie, but he knew he could make it down the hall to her bed.

He started walking. She kissed him harder, deeper. He lost track of where he was going and collided with the door frame on the way through. She groaned.

He groaned, too. "Sorry…"

"I'll live," she muttered against his mouth. "Keep walking."

And he did.

At least she'd left her bedroom door wide-open. He carried her through, turning that time, so she went in feetfirst and they could fit without running into anything.

Her bed was waiting, wide and inviting, the covers already turned back. He set her down on the white sheets. She held on. Probably afraid that if she let go of him, he would start telling her why they shouldn't do this.

She didn't have to worry. He had no arguments left. He wanted this and she did, too.

So be it.

They were doing it.

Gently, he took her hands and peeled them off his neck.

She moaned as he broke the never-ending kiss. "Ethan, don't go..." She tipped her face up to him longingly, offering those soft, tempting lips.

He took her shoulders. "Lizzie. Lizzie, open your eyes."

With great reluctance, she did. They were so soft right then, her eyes, soft and moss-green. "Don't you dare turn me down," she said in a whisper that promised everything and threatened some, too.

He laughed then, low and huskily. "I'm not turning you down."

"I mean it. This is what I want. This is..." She blinked and blew several strands of hair out of those beautiful eyes. "Uh. What did you say?"

He kissed her, quick and hard. "I said, I'm here. I'm staying. All I'm trying to do right now is take off my clothes."

Her eyes somehow got brighter. Slowly, she grinned. "You're serious. You surrender?"

"I do, yes. You win, Lizzie."

"Well, then." She blew the hair out of her eyes again. "By all means. Go right ahead and take off your clothes." She released him and scooted back among the pillows, gathering her long, bare legs up under her chin, looking about as cute as he'd ever seen her.

Plus, she was naked. That definitely added to her considerable appeal. He straightened and started stripping. He had his shirt off, his belt undone, his zipper down in seconds. He kicked off the mocs he liked to wear around the house. All that was left was to shove down his jeans and his boxers and step out of them.

She licked her lips. "Oh, Ethan…"

He started to go down to her, but then he remembered. "We need condoms."

And just like that, she reached over and pulled open the bedside drawer. "Got 'em," she said. "Plus, I'm on the pill."

He should have known. It was so like her, to take care of her own protection. Lizzie was not the kind of woman who left things to chance. Especially not something so important as a new life—or as dangerous as an STD.

Well, all right. That problem solved. He took the box from the drawer, set a couple of packets on the nightstand and then put the box back. She slid the drawer closed.

And then, finally, there was nothing else—no questions unanswered, no necessities unattended to. There was only the two of them.

Him and Lizzie. At last. Naked.

He went down to her, gathered her close in his arms. She sighed as she eagerly accepted his kiss.

She was…a miracle, in his arms. Nothing like the small, fragile women he'd always chosen. There was so much more of her, and all of it womanly and smooth and strong and sweet-smelling.

So good.

She filled his arms.

And his senses.

She rolled him over until she was on top of him and then she kissed him until he hardly knew where he was or how he'd gotten there. He only hoped he would never have to leave.

He rolled them both again, so she was on her back. He cupped her breasts in his hands. They were full and so beautiful. He kissed them. He took her nipple into his mouth and sucked on it, teasing it with his tongue, drawing on it deeply, while she wove her fingers in his hair and held him close and lifted her body toward his mouth, offering herself up.

Giving him all of her. Every glorious, long, sturdy inch.

He touched her all over, molding the inward curve of her waist, dipping his index finger into her navel and then his tongue after that. He eased his hand over her lower belly, which was smooth and slightly rounded, begging for his caress.

She lifted her hips to his hand, letting her long, strong thighs fall open. He touched her there, at the womanly heart of her. And she moved against his hand, her hips rocking, her soft mouth sighing. She said his name. She said it more than once.

As if she meant it. As if he was someone so special. The only one for her.

He kissed her. Right there, where it counted. He parted the vanilla-and-orange-scented dark gold curls and he put his mouth on her. She was wet and soft and slick and hot. He drank her in. She tasted so sweet. Sweet as heaven.

His Lizzie—and yeah, okay. She wasn't his. Not really. But that evening, together with her in that way he never had been before, it felt as if she was his.

And he was hers.

And this thing they had, this way of being that was open and true and, yeah, about sex, but also about so much more…

It was like nothing he'd ever known before with any other person. It was so special.

It meant everything to him. More than he knew how to say in words. More than he even really understood.

She reached down and she held his head as he pleasured

her, her fingers splayed in his hair. She lifted toward his secret kiss, open, ready, her body rising toward the finish so easily, so freely.

Strange. To think of Lizzie as a lover. *His* lover.

Strange. But *right,* too. Just exactly right.

"There," she whispered. "Oh, Ethan. Just…there…"

And he felt the butterfly wing fluttering against his tongue, felt her as she came, as the finish took her and rippled through her, as she cried his name yet again.

And then again.

He stayed with her. He kissed her through the soft explosions of her climax. He went on kissing her until, with a final long sigh, she lay limp under his touch.

Then he lifted his head enough to rest on her belly. She stroked his hair and traced the shape of his eyebrows, one and then the other.

And then she urged him up her body, one slim, strong arm reaching out to take a packet from the nightstand. She tore it open with her teeth.

He found that unbelievably sexy for no reason he really understood: Lizzie, placing her neat white teeth on the edge of that wrapper, tearing it open.

She eased a hand down between them. And she encircled him.

He almost choked with the thrill of that, of her cool and capable hand surrounding him.

And then she kissed him. She caught his mouth with her soft lips, and below, she was stroking him….

He knew he was going to explode. Just lose it, right then, without having felt the ultimate, longed-for, dreamed-about heat of her body surrounding him.

But somehow, he held on. Held out.

And after a long, wet kiss and numberless glorious and almost unbearable slow strokes with her clever hand, she finally lowered the condom between them, positioned it and rolled it carefully down over him.

He knew then that he would make it. He could hold out long enough to be inside her at last.

"Lizzie." He whispered her name.

She opened her eyes and met his gaze. She looked dazed, gone, lost in this impossible moment. She looked like *he* felt.

He smiled. And she responded with a slight lifting at the corners of her red, wet mouth.

"Now?" he asked.

She nodded. And she held his gaze as she wrapped her legs around him and guided him home.

He sank into her with a low groan. She welcomed him, lifting herself, opening.

Nothing like it. Ever. In bed with Lizzie, her slim arms and her long legs around him.

He gave it up to her. He buried his face in the curve of her sweet-scented throat. He rocked his hips against her in a slow, perfect glide.

She went with him. She took his every thrust and gave it back to him. She was like no other woman he had ever known.

She was all the good things, the strong things, the *real* things.

She was everything.

And more.

Later, he kissed every bruise on her body, lingering over the really big, angry-looking one at the base of her spine.

Then they got up and went upstairs to his rooms—and the master bath, where the jetted tub was big enough for two and then some. They soaked for a while.

And they made love again.

And then, around eight-thirty, they both decided they were starving. He gave her a flannel shirt to wear and he pulled on some old sweats. They went down to the kitchen where they ate leftover lasagna.

They talked a little, sitting at the kitchen table. They agreed that they would just enjoy these last days together, really *be* together in every way.

There would be no worrying about the future.

He still felt a little guilty, though. Lizzie was his friend. He knew her goals included a good marriage and eventually babies. He was not going to be the guy who put a ring on her finger.

He admitted, "I really feel like I'm taking advantage of you."

And Lizzie threw back her head and laughed. "No, you are not. You are showing me how to live in the now and I plan to love every moment of it. So shut up and stop trying to be noble."

He felt vaguely offended. "Trying? I'm only *trying?*"

"Well, if you were really going to *be* noble, you wouldn't have let me seduce you today."

He found that totally unfair. "Lizzie, you came out into the kitchen, all pink and sweet from a bath, with your hair curling and wild-looking just the way I know you know I like it. You were wearing only a *towel.*"

"Yes, I was, wasn't I?" She looked downright proud of herself.

"And then you dropped the towel."

"You liked that, did you?"

"Lizzie, I'm only a man."

"Yes, you are." She raised her water glass. "And a very good man, I must say. A wonderful man."

He grunted. "How can I get annoyed with you when you call me wonderful?"

"You can't." She set her glass down. "Let it be, Ethan. It is what it is. Let's enjoy the time we have together."

It was good advice. *Great* advice.

So why couldn't he shake the feeling that in the end, when it was over, she wasn't going to just give it up and walk away? Why couldn't he shake the feeling that she wanted more from him than to be her lover for the next eleven days, that she wanted more than he had it in him to give?

She shoved back her chair and started unbuttoning the shirt she'd borrowed from him. "Ethan." Slowly, she peeled the shirt wide. He saw her pretty breasts and her soft belly and that little patch of curly, tempting hair down low.

"That's not fair," he said darkly.

"Stop thinking. Enjoy." She shrugged the shirt off her shoulders and let it fall to the floor.

He swore. And then he got up and went around the table and took her in his arms.

They were still in bed the next morning when Bonnie Drake called. Lizzie lay back on the pillow next to Ethan and listened to the Realtor tell her that Aubert Pelletier had accepted her offer.

Lizzie's mind started spinning. It was happening! It was real. She owned a bakery!

Bonnie said something else about the inspections and all they had to get done before the closing on July fifth. As if Lizzie could think of anything else right that moment but the one, shining fact that her cherished dream was finally coming true.

She thanked Bonnie politely.

"I'll need your earnest-money check right away,"

Bonnie reminded her. Earnest money was a good-faith deposit on her down payment.

"Of course," Lizzie said. "I'll bring it by. Um, say, one this afternoon?"

"That will work. I'll be here at the office then."

She thanked Bonnie again. They said goodbye. Lizzie turned off the phone and, staring dazedly at the ceiling, reached out and dropped it on the nightstand.

"Well?" Ethan rose on an elbow and leaned over her. His hair was rumpled and his eyes were lazy. His bare chest and shoulders were big and broad and tempting as the rest of him.

She reached up, slid her hand around his neck and pulled him down for a long, wet kiss.

When she finally let him go, she said it out loud for the first time. "I just bought myself a bakery."

They got up eventually, had a very late breakfast and then drove to Thunder Creek Realty to deliver the earnest-money check.

After that, they went to Bozeman, where Ethan met with some ranchers about more oil-shale leases. They got back to the house after six.

She had her girls' night out with Erin and the group at seven. She rushed to get ready while Ethan called Dillon and Corey and the other men whose wives would be out with Lizzie that evening. He invited them all over to play poker.

DJ, Dax and Dillon had babysitting duty. Ethan said they should bring the little ones over. He would make them popcorn and they could watch Disney movies on the DVR.

Lizzie kissed him goodbye at the door, a very long kiss, one that left her giddy and yearning. She found herself kind of wondering why she was going out when she could be home with him.

But then she met all her Thunder Canyon girlfriends at the Hitching Post and she totally got it. A surprise love affair with Ethan was a very special thing, but girlfriends mattered, too. They mattered a lot.

Every one of those wonderful women hooted and hollered and clapped and jumped up and down when she told them that she'd bought La Boulangerie.

Allaire said, "I knew it."

And Tori just grinned.

Steph Clifton asked, "Are you changing the name—and when are you opening?"

"It will be the Mountain Bluebell Bakery," Lizzie announced. She could tell by the gleam in Steph's eyes that she remembered that moment up on Thunder Mountain, when Lizzie had seen the blue thimble-shaped flowers and Steph had told her what they were called.

"I like it," said Steph, with feeling. She raised her tall glass of tonic with lime high. "To Lizzie and the Mountain Bluebell Bakery. Much success."

"To Lizzie," the others echoed. "To Lizzie and her bakery…"

"And what about your grand opening?" Allaire wanted to know. "You didn't say when."

Lizzie hardly dared to admit her plan. She knew she was probably being unrealistic, so she started hedging. "I know this will sound impossible, but the equipment is all in place. If there are no surprises, we're pretty much ready to go. I know there will be a mountain of permits to get, some kind of a promotional campaign to plan. And I'll have to hire and train at least a couple of employees, just to get the doors open. But I did practically grow up in a bakery. I know what needs doing and I know how to do it. I have all my mother's time-tested recipes and they are fantastic. And I've had my basic business plan worked out and ready to go for years now."

"But when?" Erin demanded. "We want to know *when*."

Lizzie confessed, "I'm shooting for the last Saturday in July."

There was more applause, more stomping and fist pumping and excited whistles. They all told her she could make it, and they promised to help any way they could.

It was a great evening, Lizzie thought, one she would always remember. It meant so much, not only to have actually bought her bakery at last, but also to have friends who believed in her, who offered unstinting encouragement and a boatload of support.

She had so much fun that she stayed out until well after midnight with the diehards of the party for that evening: Shandie Traub, Hayley Cates and Erin and Tori. Erin wouldn't let Lizzie buy a round or even a plate of nachos the whole night. "This is my tiny little payback," she insisted. "For my beautiful, perfect wedding cake."

The house was dark when Lizzie got back. The poker game must have ended, the players and the little ones they'd brought with them all gone home.

When she came through the inner door of the garage, she could see the faint glow from the kitchen, the under-counter lights that they always left on during the night. But everything was very quiet.

Ethan must be in bed. She seriously considered tiptoeing up the stairs and joining him. But really, the poor man probably needed his sleep. She'd kept him up most of the night last night—and before that, there'd been all the excitement up on Thunder Mountain during the day.

Uh-uh. He deserved a break. She went on down the hall to her own room, where she quietly shut the door and got undressed.

The soft knock came when she stood by the bed in her panties and matching camisole. She felt a definite rising sensation under her breastbone and her pulse sped up.

So he wasn't asleep, after all.

She padded over and pulled open the door and there he was, barefoot and bare-chested in a pair of frayed sweats that rode low on his hips.

"I heard the garage door open," he said, his eyes full of promises she fully intended to see that he kept.

"I didn't want to wake you…" She was whispering, moving in nice and close. He drew her like a magnet. She wanted his touch, his kiss, his body heat.

He did touch her. He ran the back of his index finger down her cheek, setting off sparks of desire, making her breath catch. "I wasn't asleep. I was waiting for you."

"Ah." It was more a sigh than an actual word.

He slipped his warm fingers under her hair and wrapped them around the back of her neck. "Did you have fun with the girls?"

"I did. So much fun." She couldn't have resisted if she'd wanted to. She leaned in, brushed a kiss across his lips.

Electric. Amazing. Every nerve in her body seemed to be purring.

He settled his mouth more firmly over hers. "Lizzie," he said against her lips. Just that. Just her name. So softly. So intently.

And then his tongue was there, tracing the shape of her mouth, leaving a trail of wet and heat. She opened. He slipped his tongue in as he gathered her closer.

They kissed, standing there in the open doorway. They kissed for a long, sweet time.

And then he undressed her. That didn't take long. He slid down the panties, pulled up the camisole and tossed it to the floor. She helped, too. She pushed down those sweats he was wearing. He kicked them away.

And she thought, as he sank to his knees before her, that she didn't want to lose him. She couldn't stand the thought of that, even though she knew that too soon, she *would* lose him.

Too soon, she would move out. And he would move on. She had accepted that. Or so she kept telling herself, so she had told him last night when he tried to get her to talk about it.

No, she didn't want to talk about it. Talking would ruin everything. As soon as they started talking, it would all become too clear. That she *did* want his ring on her finger.

She wanted it a lot. She wanted Ethan for a lifetime.

And Ethan for a lifetime was something no other woman had managed to get. A lifetime was something he just didn't want to share.

She sighed and she gazed down through half-closed eyes at his dark head. He parted her with those clever fingers. He kissed her there, at the heart of her sex. It felt so good. So right.

Good enough that she moaned and speared her fingers in his hair and let her head fall back. Good enough that she forgot everything but the moment, everything but the silky feel of his dark hair between her fingers, everything but his hot mouth against her, and the fire building within.

A few minutes later, he scooped her up and carried her, limp and satisfied and yet longing for more, to the bed. As he gently lowered her to the sheets, she told herself that whatever happened later, it was worth it. To be with him like this, just the two of them. For a little while.

As a man and a woman.

In the middle of the night.

Chapter Thirteen

Each day was a treasure.

Every night like a sweet, naughty dream.

It all fled by much too fast. In the last week of June, they spent Monday morning dealing with inspections—both for Ethan's new office building and for Lizzie's bakery. Both buildings required some minor repairs and those were scheduled to be handled within that week.

Monday afternoon, at a local car lot, Lizzie bought a barely used Chevy cargo van with all-wheel drive. It had only ten thousand miles on it. She was thrilled to have found it, because she was not only going to need her own vehicle, but she was also going to need one with plenty of space for hauling goods to and from the bakery. Ethan had the rental place pick up the economy car she'd been using and she parked the van in the garage.

Tuesday and Wednesday they were on the road meeting face-to-face with more ranchers and landowners, following new leads Ethan had turned up. Thursday, Ethan's mom and stepdad flew in. They spent the rest of that day and Friday, too, at the resort finalizing the investment that TOI had decided to make. To represent TOI's interest, Ethan assumed a seat on the Thunder Canyon Resort Group board.

Saturday, Rose arrived in town for a monthlong vacation. She took a luxury suite in the clubhouse at the resort, confiding to Lizzie that she liked to be where the action was. Allaire had a family party out at her and DJ's ranch that night. Ethan and Lizzie went together—and the strangest thing happened: nothing.

No one seemed to notice that they were together in a different way than before. Probably because it wasn't anything all that new in a social setting for him to spend a lot of time talking with her, or to throw his arm around her shoulders in a companionable sort of way. Over the years, she'd often stood in as his "date" for parties and family gatherings. He'd always said he liked going out with her. She was fun, he said. And he felt relaxed around her. Plus, she never clung or acted needy, unlike some of his girlfriends.

At home in his bed that night they joked about it, that they were having a hot affair, and no one had a clue.

But in her heart, Lizzie was starting to wonder if it might have been the two of them who didn't have a clue. They had never realized what they actually were to each other, that they were more than just friends, more even, than lovers.

And they'd both been blind to the truth for too long.

Now, she had the blinders off. She knew that she loved him. But he had never once so much as hinted that he might love her.

So did that mean he was hiding his true feelings from her?

She wanted to think so. But then again, what would be the point? He knew that she wanted a home and a family. If he wanted that, too, and with her, well, why not just ask her? Some men were shy about going after what they wanted.

But not Ethan. No way.

Which led her right back to the original problem, to the most likely truth: she loved him and she'd started picturing a life with him.

And he just wanted what he'd always wanted: to have a good time and to be free.

She told herself not to think about it. She promised herself she would enjoy what they had right now. And then she would let him go. She told herself it was good for her, to just go for it for once in her life, to live in the moment and not always be thinking ahead, always worrying about what was going to happen next.

And then she realized that she was doing just what she'd told herself this one time she wouldn't—worrying about the future.

Monday, Independence Day, the day before the fifth of July, came much too soon.

It was a big day in Thunder Canyon, with a parade down Main Street and a Fourth of July rodeo out at the fairgrounds. And then, that evening, there was the Independence Day dance upstairs in the ballroom of the town hall.

Ethan insisted they do it all. They watched the parade, went to the rodeo, had dinner at the Rib Shack with half of the town. And then, in the evening, they went to the dance.

It was a casual kind of thing, the women in summer dresses and the men in jeans, Western shirts and boots.

Lizzie and Ethan danced to the six-piece band up on the stage at the far end of the rustic, wood-paneled ballroom. She also found time to hang out with her friends. Everyone wanted to know about her progress with the bakery. She told them that she was closing the sale the next day. And she'd be moving into the apartment above the shop before the end of the week.

They were all so sweet and encouraging. Anything she needed, they reminded her, she only had to let them know.

At ten, out on Main Street, the town merchants put on a fireworks display. Everyone piled out onto the ballroom balcony or down the stairs and outside to watch the show. She and Ethan managed to squeeze into a corner of the balcony. There were fountains and spinners and those rockets that rose with a high, screaming sound and exploded into huge, varicolored pinwheels of light high in the clear night sky.

Ethan whispered in her ear, "Now aren't you glad you gave in and came with me to Montana?"

She answered without hesitation. "Oh, yeah." No matter what happened—or didn't happen—between the two of them, she was happy she had come here, happy to be calling Thunder Canyon her home.

"Let's dance," he said a few minutes later, after the last bright fountain of flame had lit up the night. He led her back inside and took her in his arms.

She surrendered to the moment then. To the feel of his big body pressed close to hers, to the touch of his hand at the small of her back. She thought of the years she had been with him and how fast, in retrospect, they had flown by.

Too soon, the night was over.

They went home to his house, to his bed. They made

love and it was sweet and hot and perfect. Then he pulled her close.

They slept. Together. For the last time.

In the morning, they each had a closing to go to. His was at ten and hers at eleven, both in the same title company's conference room. Ethan stayed on after he closed on his office building to be there for Lizzie when she signed the endless series of papers finalizing her sale.

By noon that day, she owned her bakery.

Ethan had agreed to meet some business associates for a late lunch in Bozeman. He wanted her to come with him. She said she couldn't. She had a million things to do.

"I'll see you around five or so, then?" he asked so easily. As if he'd totally forgotten that today was the last day, the day they'd agreed to say goodbye.

So, had the fact that it was ending between them just slipped his mind? That seemed impossible. But then again, Ethan could be oblivious when it came to personal relationships, especially when he didn't want to face what was happening.

Or maybe he did remember. And he was fine with it.

They were standing on the sidewalk outside the title company offices. It was neither the time nor the place to ask him if he happened to remember that she was leaving him that day.

So she forced a smile and leaned close to brush a quick kiss against his warm lips. "See you at five."

At the house, she longed to head for the kitchen and start baking. She felt so awful about leaving him and baking would have soothed her.

But no. She really was going. Today, as she'd planned.

She started packing. It didn't take all that long. Most of her stuff was still in Midland, in storage, and at Ethan's house there. She'd already made arrangements to have it all shipped to the shop. The apartment upstairs was fully furnished. Aubert Pelletier had given her a great price on not only the shop, all its contents and the building, but also the contents of the living quarters. She would have no problem getting by until the bulk of her things arrived next week.

Because she knew that Ethan wouldn't be back for hours yet, she put everything in her van and drove on over to Main Street, where she lugged her suitcases up the stairs and put all her clothes away in the larger bedroom at the back of the building.

So strange to imagine herself living here. She felt kind of numb at the prospect. Her dream was finally coming true and it felt just a little *too* much like a dream—meaning slightly unreal.

But it was going to happen. She *would* be sleeping here. Tonight, as a matter of fact.

She stood at the window that looked out over Main Street and thought again how charming and homey Thunder Canyon was. It was going to be fine. It was all going to work out perfectly.

And for right now, it was best to keep moving. To do what needed doing. To leave no time for wishing that certain things could be different, no time for brooding over the fact that tonight was not only her first night in the apartment, but it was also the night she would have to find a way to say goodbye to the man she loved.

She went into the kitchen where she plugged in the refrigerator and went through all the cabinets. Thanks to Aubert Pelletier's willingness to leave so much behind, she had all the basics: dishes, flatware, utensils, pots and pans.

She had no linens, though. She should have thought of that. And she would also need food. So she grabbed her keys and headed over to the JCPenney in the New Town Mall, where she loaded up a shopping cart with a mattress cover, pillows, sheets and blankets in addition to towels and washcloths and the like. After Penney's, she stopped in at a supermarket to stock up on food and sundries.

At the apartment, she lugged the linens to the small service porch off the kitchen. She stuck the sheets in the washer half of the stacked washer/dryer and started the cycle. Then she made three more trips up and down the stairs, hauling in the groceries. She put everything away, transferred the sheets to the dryer and stuck the towels in the washer.

By then it was almost five and she knew that Ethan would be back at the house anytime now. She wanted to be there when he arrived. To thank him for everything.

To maybe, just possibly, try to get up the courage to say what was in her heart—yes, she knew he was a total commitment-phobe. But still, it didn't seem right to walk away without telling him exactly how she felt about him.

And then, if telling him she loved him changed nothing, to wish him well. And say goodbye.

She returned to the house.

When the garage door rumbled up, she saw that his SUV was already inside. Her heart lurched at the sight.

One big fat moment of truth, coming right up.

As she jumped down from the van, the inside door to the house opened. "Don't you ever answer your cell?" Ethan demanded in a tone that wasn't exactly angry, but close. "I got home at four. And I called you twice."

She shut the door to the van and fumbled in her purse until she found her cell. *Two missed calls.* "I'm sorry. I just didn't hear it ringing. And you know, sometimes, with all the mountains around, there are dead spots. The calls don't get through when you make them. It's possible that the phone never did ring and I…" Sheesh. She was babbling. She needed to stop that.

"You what?" He stepped back so she could enter.

"Never mind. I'm sorry, all right? I'm just…sorry."

For that, she got nothing. He waited for her to come in. She did. She crossed the threshold and then she hesitated. Where to go? After all, she didn't live there anymore.

And he was not helping. All he did was shut the door and stand there some more. So she turned and started walking until she reached her favorite place in any house.

The kitchen.

She went to the table, pulled out her usual chair and sat down.

He hung back in the doorway, looking distinctly suspicious. "Okay, Lizzie," he said finally. "What's going on?"

She bit her lip. "Ethan, I…" The words just wouldn't come.

"Your apron," he accused. "It's missing." He marched over, opened the pantry door and pointed at the empty hook on the back of it. "And I went to your room. Everything of yours is gone."

She gave a wimpy little sweep of her hand toward the chair across from her. "Come on, sit down. Please."

He looked at her as if he wouldn't mind strangling her. "You moved out. Just like that. While I was in Bozeman."

"Ethan, we agreed that—"

He put up a hand. "Uh-uh. Don't give me that. We talked about it almost two weeks ago. Once. Nothing specific was said."

"That's not so. We agreed—"

"—today would be your last day working for me, yeah. But that's all. You never once mentioned you were just going to pack your stuff and go."

Softly, she asked, "What exactly did you think I would do?"

"Not this." He shut the pantry door. Hard. "Not this, that's for damn sure."

She had no idea where to go from there. Nothing she might have said seemed right or appropriate. So she just sat there, mute, wondering if maybe the thing to do was to simply get up and go.

Finally, he came toward her in long strides. Her pulse accelerated. She really had no idea where this was going.

But then he only yanked out his chair and dropped into it. "All right. I'm sitting. Talk."

"Ethan, come on…"

He only glared at her. "Talk."

"I just… I'm sorry. I truly am. I didn't want it to turn out like this. But it's only that I, well, I can't…" Lord, she was making a hash of this.

Apparently, he thought so, too. He made a scoffing sound. "You can't what?"

Say it, a brave voice in her head commanded. *Just tell him. Get it over with.* "I… Look. I've tried, okay? I've really tried. To…live in the moment. To just be with you and not think about where what we have is going. Because I know you. I know what you want out of life and it's not what I want."

He braced both forearms on the table and loomed closer, still glaring. "You're not telling me anything I don't already know."

"Ethan, you're acting really strange. Huffing around. Slamming doors. It's not like you at all."

He sat back in the chair and let out a slow, careful breath. He looked away, then back at her again. Now, in his eyes she saw hurt. He was hurt that she was leaving him.

The last thing she'd wanted was to hurt him.

He said, "You know it's not over with us." Now his voice was low and soft. Too soft. "Everything's been going great. I don't get it, that's all. Why walk out on a good thing?"

Tell him. Do it. Say it now. "I love you, Ethan." She said the words and she instantly wanted to take them back, but she didn't. She pushed ahead, eager to finish it, to get it all out there, to give him the truth as she knew it. "I'm *in* love with you. Yes, I've had a great time these past couple of weeks, but I want a lot more from you than a really good time. I want to marry you. I want you for the rest of our lives."

"Oh." He gulped. Yes, he did. He actually gulped. She watched in despair as his Adam's apple bounced up and then down. And then he coughed into his hand.

Lizzie didn't know whether to burst into hysterical laughter or break down in tears. Somehow, she managed to do neither. She held it together. "I don't want to be just your girlfriend for a little while longer. Until you get tired of me. Until you're ready to move on. I'd rather have it end now, when it's still good between us. I'd rather walk away with a little dignity. I'd rather spare us both all the crap that happens later, when it's finally just too painfully obvious that I want more than you want and we can't deny that anymore. So I'm just telling you right out that I'm in love with you and I've had such a beautiful, magical time, living in the moment with you. But you know, I've learned that I just can't go on with this anymore, that living in the moment doesn't work for me. Not unless the moment is connected to an endless chain of moments. A lifetime of moments of you and me, together, building a future, making a family."

He spoke in a ragged voice. "Married. My God. It's not like I didn't know it. I did know it." He rubbed the bridge of his nose between his thumb and forefinger.

Was she giving him a headache? It sure looked as if she was.

She felt a little insulted. And a little sorry for him. But mostly, she just loved him and wished that this could be over. Or that there had been some better, more graceful way to do this.

"Well?" he demanded. "Just tell me. If I said right now that I would marry you, would you stay?"

"No," she said simply. Because she *didn't* want marriage. Not like this. No way.

"But you just said—"

"Ethan. Stop."

"But I don't—"

"Seriously, stop. Remember that night I told you that you were being an ass?"

His eyes narrowed. He muttered, "Yeah. I remember."

"Well, you're doing it again, okay? Stop."

He raked his fingers back through his hair and said a few bad words in quick succession. "I would do it. All right? I would marry you. That's how I feel right now. I would marry you to keep you with me. I would do anything. Just about any damn thing you said I had to do. Because…you do it for me, Lizzie. You do it for me in every way. And if marriage is what you need to make it work for you, well, okay. Marriage it will be, then."

Lizzie only stared at him. How strange. He was offering her what she wanted most, and yet there was no way, under these circumstances, that she could accept his proposition.

He shot her a hot, fuming glance. "Well? Don't sit there looking at me like I just shot your dog. What do you say?"

She held his eyes. She refused to look away. "I already said it. No. No way. I happen to believe in marriage, Ethan. I believe in two people, together, making the best life they can. I believe in love and commitment and a white dress and a diamond ring. I believe in *you,* and that's the God's truth. And I believe you're better than this."

Her tears clogged her throat now. They couldn't be stopped. Her nose was hot and her eyes were burning. The salty wetness broke the dam of her lower eyelids and trailed slowly down her cheek. She swiped them away. And then she shoved back her chair, went to the counter and whipped a few tissues from the box waiting there.

He was still sitting where she'd left him, watching her, his eyes dark and haunted. And then he started to rise. "Don't cry, Lizzie. Damn it. Don't cry."

"No!" She stuck out a hand. "Don't, okay? Just…don't."

He sank back into the chair.

She blew her nose, dried her cheeks, turned to toss the soggy tissues in the trash bin under the sink. Finally, when she turned to him again, she brought up her hands and pressed the cool tips of her fingers against her eyelids.

He said, "It's only…I came home and you weren't here. And I *knew,* you know? I knew that you were moving out. I wasn't surprised, but I was pissed off all of a sudden. I was just really mad. Lizzie, I don't get this. You. Me. This whole thing. I, well, I like my life the way it is. But then, I think of my life without you and I hate it. You know?"

She did know. She knew too well.

Slowly, she lowered her hands from her face and met his gaze. And then she told him, her voice barely above a whisper, "I can't say yes to you when you don't even know if my saying yes is what you really want. That would be wrong, all wrong, for both of us. There has to be…joy in it, Ethan. You have to come to me with your mind and your heart wide-open."

All his previous anger was gone now. He only looked hurt and confused. And in his eyes she saw his longing.

For her. For what they had together. For the years of true friendship. And for the last few brief, glorious days when there had been so much more. "I...don't know how to give you what you want, Lizzie. I don't know how to be that guy. Not everybody's like you. Not everybody wants to settle down and live happily ever after."

Her eyes were dry by then. She understood what she had to do.

She went to him. He watched her approach, his gaze wary and yet somehow tender, too. When she stood above him, she took his handsome face in her two hands and she bent down close. She pressed her lips to his.

He sighed against her mouth. "Lizzie..." But at least he didn't reach for her.

She made herself straighten to her height again. She made herself step back from him, moving over to the chair she had left, dipping to grab her bag and settle it over her shoulder. "Goodbye, Ethan."

He said nothing.

She passed in front of him to get to the door. He didn't try to stop her.

And that, she told herself, was for the best. She went out the way she had come in, through the garage, opening the outer door with the button on the wall, taking the remote opener out of her van and leaving it on the front passenger seat of his SUV, where he would see it the next time he used the car.

She got in the van, started it up, backed down the driveway and headed for Old Town. Her new life was waiting for her.

Too bad her chest felt hollow, echoing with emptiness. As if she'd torn out her heart and left it behind.

Chapter Fourteen

The next day, Ethan's new assistant arrived from Midland. Her name was Kay Bausch. Kay was fifty-two and had been with TOI for over two decades, assisting several different executives in various departments. She was smart and efficient, a widow who'd wanted a new start in a different town. She took an apartment in a complex in New Town and went to work right away, setting up shop in the new office building on State Street.

Ethan didn't look for a housekeeper at first. He couldn't bear the thought of having to see some other woman in the kitchen, doing what Lizzie had always done, the cooking. The cleaning up.

But within a week, the house started looking really bad. He kept thinking he would clean the damn place up himself. But he was working long hours, getting TOI Montana going, and traveling around the state a lot. Eventually, he had to accept that he possessed neither the time nor the inclination to whip the place back into shape.

He lucked out when he went to dinner at Tori and Connor McFarlane's on the second Wednesday of the month. Tori told him that her housekeeper had a sister who was looking for a steady housekeeping job. The woman's children were grown, but there was a husband. She didn't want to live in, which was fine with Ethan. He didn't want some stranger living in Lizzie's rooms anyway.

Her name was Norma Stahl. She came the next morning. She was quiet and she worked fast. When she left that evening, the house was spotless and there was meat loaf in the oven.

It was nine days since Lizzie had left him. And he'd already succeeded in finding her replacements both at home and on the job. He had a very capable assistant and a pleasant, hardworking housekeeper. Things could have been worse.

Or so he kept trying to tell himself.

If only he didn't miss Lizzie every moment of every day. If only he didn't feel so damn lonely. If only life without Lizzie hadn't turned out even worse than he'd thought it was going to be.

Allaire had him over for dinner that Friday. Casually, his cousin's wife mentioned that she'd seen Lizzie several times in the past few days. Lizzie had hired Allaire to paint the new sign that would go over the bakery door. And the place was really coming together—new paint, new light fixtures, that sort of thing. Lizzie had hired someone to help on the counter and was training someone else to assist her with the baking.

"She's an amazing woman," Allaire added.

As if he didn't damn well know that. As if he even needed to hear all that stuff about how well she was doing, how everyone in town just couldn't wait until her grand opening.

Had he seen the ads she'd put in the *Thunder Canyon Nugget?* Cute, weren't they? Really eye-catching.

Allaire modestly admitted that she had designed them.

He left his cousin's house at nine that night, earlier than he should have, he knew. Leaving so early was borderline rude, but he had to get out of there.

Lizzie this. Lizzie that.

It was driving him crazy.

He headed for the Hitching Post, thinking maybe he'd meet someone, a pretty, big-eyed woman, someone delicate and sweet. But when he got there, he couldn't go in. He sat in the parking lot for a while, feeling like a wuss, wondering what had happened to him. And then he started up the SUV again and got out of there.

It didn't seem right to try to forget Lizzie in some strange woman's arms. If that made him a wuss, so be it.

The bakery just happened to be on his way home. He drove right on by, not slowing or stopping. He wasn't that bad off, he told himself. No so bad off that he would hang around her place, just hoping for a glimpse of her. But still, he couldn't help glancing up at the second story as he passed.

The lights were on in the apartment. He thought he saw her shadow move behind the drawn shades. Was she alone?

It hurt bad to think that she might not be. But then, he was already hurting. Hurting with missing her. He was beginning to see that she had filled a hole he hadn't even known was there in his world. In his life.

A hole he only recognized as an emptiness now that she was gone.

He went back to the house, where it hurt to go inside

and smell nothing but a faint hint of lemon wax, which Norma used when she dusted. No muffins, blueberry or otherwise. No butter-pecan sugar cookies. No strawberry-rhubarb pie.

No Lizzie in her old blue robe, her hair wild on the sides and flattened at the back of her head, offering a drink or a hot cup of decaf.

He poured his own drink. A big one. And he sat in the easy chair in the family room. He sipped and he brooded.

He considered certain facts that he'd been avoiding admitting. Like how Lizzie provided everything a man could ever want from a woman; she created a place to call home where otherwise there was nothing but a lonely house. She gave him muffins in the morning—or whenever he wanted them. From her, he got straight talk and a few laughs, too. She told him the truth always. Nothing less.

And then there was the sex. It was terrific with Lizzie. Better than just good. She made love like she baked—with her whole heart.

He shook his head. Come on, what was he doing?

The point was to get over her. To get over her and get on with his life. He couldn't do that if he kept looking back, kept going over all the things he missed about her now that she was gone.

Right then and there, he made a silent vow not to think about Lizzie anymore. It wasn't the first time he'd made such a vow.

They never lasted, those particular vows, because seriously, how does a man make himself *not* think about a woman?

He only ended up thinking about how he *wasn't* going to think about her. Which, when you came right down to it, still counted as thinking about her.

Ethan dropped his head to the chair back and glared at the ceiling. What a damn mess.

None of this was working out the way he'd planned.

The next day, Saturday, he drove to Great Falls. He had dinner with a landowner who had agreed to lease him mineral rights. And he had a reservation at the same motel he and Lizzie had stayed in back in June.

He ended up getting back in his SUV and driving home because the motel reminded him of Lizzie.

Which was downright pitiful, if he really thought about it.

He kept good and busy through the third week in July. He flew down to Midland Monday for a series of meetings at TOI. He had dinner with his mom and Pete twice during the three-day visit. They each made a point to get him aside and ask him if he was all right.

He told them both that he was fine. Great. Perfect. He had it all. The resort investment was a solid one. TOI Montana was a go. Things couldn't be better.

Did either of them believe him? He had no clue. He told himself it was nice that they cared, but he wished they would just mind their own damn business.

He got back to Thunder Canyon Thursday and there were a million things to do at the office. He got on top of that as best he could.

Sunday, he went with Corey and Erin to the same church they'd been married in. Afterward, Erin fixed them a big lunch at her and Corey's new house.

Erin, like most of the women in town, had become good friends with Lizzie. Ethan felt a little edgy the whole afternoon, waiting for Erin to start in about how wonderful Lizzie was.

But Erin didn't even mention Lizzie's name.

For some reason, his sister-in-law's silence on the subject of the woman he couldn't stop thinking about irked him even more than if she'd gone ahead and babbled about Lizzie constantly.

After lunch, Corey suggested the two of them retreat to his study. They refilled their coffee cups and went into Corey's office at the front of the house.

Corey gestured at one of the leather easy chairs in a grouping near the tall front windows. "I gotta ask. You all right?"

Ethan sat down and put his coffee on a waiting coaster. "What the hell kind of question is that?"

Corey went over and shut the door before taking the other chair. "You seem edgy. Like any minute you're going to bite someone's head off."

"I'm fine, got it? Fine." He grabbed his coffee, took another sip.

Corey shook his head. "Whatever you say."

"I mean, why shouldn't I be fine? I've got it all."

"You certainly have."

"I should be happy as a bull in high clover."

Corey just looked at him.

"What?" he demanded.

And Corey did it. He said it out loud. "Well, yeah. You've got it all—except for Lizzie. You let *her* go."

Ethan considered how satisfying it would be to jump up, haul his brother out of that fat leather chair and bust him a good one right in the chops.

Corey knew it, too. "Think about it. What good is it going to do you to hit me?"

Ethan waved a hand and mumbled, "None. No good at all, but it's still tempting."

"You're in love with Lizzie, aren't you?" Corey asked the question gently.

For several seconds, Ethan refused to answer. He scowled at the far wall. But in the end, he came out with it. "Yeah."

"So why did you let her go?"

He blew out a hard breath. "She really wants that bakery. I tried to hold her back at first, for my own selfish reasons. But the more I found out how much she means to me, the more I wanted her to have it, to have everything she ever wanted."

Corey made a snorting sound. "I'm not talking about the bakery, you idiot. I'm talking about you and her and what you've got together. The whole family—the whole *town*—knows how you feel about her. *And* how she feels about you. What you two have together is a rare thing. I'm asking you why you wanted to let that go."

Ethan groaned. "You're serious? The whole town knows?"

Corey only gave him a long, patient look.

Finally, Ethan told him, "Lizzie's a forever kind of woman. And you know me, I get nervous when a woman starts getting serious."

"You keep telling yourself that long enough, you're bound to make it true no matter what."

"What the hell is that supposed to mean?"

"It means that you and Lizzie have it all. You started out working together, then you became the best of friends. And then, over time...more. How long has it been since you were with another woman?"

Ethan shot his brother a lowering glance. "What kind of question is that?"

"Just answer it. How long?"

"I don't know. Six months, maybe—no, wait. Seven."

"There's been no one else in the last seven months."

"Didn't I just say that?"

"I was only making sure."

Ethan muttered darkly, "I hope you're going somewhere important with this."

"Have you been *thinking* about going out with someone else since you and Lizzie called it quits?"

Ethan picked up his coffee cup and plunked it down without drinking from it. "No, all right? No, I don't feel like going out with anyone else. And is there a point you're getting to here?"

"Well, I'm only saying that it seems to me that you're not acting like the player you keep insisting you are. Not anymore. You're acting like a man who is serious over one particular woman. A man in love, which you have just admitted to me you are. A man who's finally found someone so right for him that he doesn't need to keep looking anymore. You've got all you want in Lizzie. But you're so thickheaded that you went and sent her away."

Ethan opened his mouth to argue but then he shut it without a word. Why fight the truth? Corey had him nailed. He'd finally found the woman for him and Lizzie was that woman. It had taken him five years of knowing her to realize what he really wanted from her.

Not someone to run his office. Not someone to keep his house. Not someone to bake his muffins or make sure his dinner was in the oven.

What he wanted from Lizzie was…Lizzie. Just Lizzie.

He wanted to spend his life with her.

And yet he had turned her down when she'd offered him everything.

He asked his brother in a voice rough with emotions he was only now starting to face, "You think she might take me back?"

Corey grunted. "You'll never know unless you try."

* * *

At eight o'clock Monday morning, the twenty-fifth of July, one week before her grand opening, Lizzie stood at the window in her living room and gazed down on Main Street. She sipped her morning coffee and felt a definite flutter of excitement in the pit of her stomach.

Five days from now. On Saturday morning, I'll be opening the doors. It will be my first day, my grand-opening day...

It seemed like a miracle, that it was really happening. There had been a thousand things to accomplish, and swiftly. Just getting all the necessary inspections and permits had been close to impossible, but she had done it. By driving herself relentlessly, every day, dawn to dark, she was making it happen. She would be ready on time.

Yeah, okay. Her heart might be hurting. Every day without Ethan was a day with a sad little empty spot in the middle of it. But sometimes a woman just had to move on. And she was doing that. She had a lot to be grateful for: good friends, a beautiful little town to live in and her dream of her bakery at last coming true. She was determined to focus on the good things, of which there were plenty.

Lizzie sniffed. With the heel of her hand, she brushed off the two lonely tears that had slid down her cheeks. It was okay, she told herself. Okay to cry a little. Sometimes a few tears helped to ease the pain.

And then she gasped.

A big SUV was driving by on the street below. Her heart bounced to her throat and her pulse started racing: Ethan.

She said the beloved name aloud. "Oh, Ethan..."

But he didn't stop. He drove on by. From her angle at the window above him, she couldn't tell if he glanced up toward where she stood, if he noticed the beautiful sign

Allaire had made for her, hung just as she'd pictured it, by iron-lace hooks above the shop door.

She leaned close to the window so she could watch until the SUV turned a corner and disappeared. And when it was gone, she rested her forehead against the glass. More tears fell. She wiped them away and was just about to go grab a tissue when she saw the small, black-haired woman coming up the street from Pine. The woman was not familiar. Lizzie couldn't recall ever seeing her before.

She stopped in front of the shop. She stared up at the sign over the door, a strange, stricken look on her heart-shaped face.

After a moment or two, she started to walk away. But then she stopped, turned decisively on her delicate high heels and marched to the shop door.

The door buzzer sounded in the apartment.

Lizzie frowned. She wasn't expecting anyone. And the sign in the window made it clear she wasn't open for business yet.

The buzzer went off again. Lizzie turned, set down her coffee and headed for the door that led out to the stairs, grabbing a tissue from the box on a side table as she flew by.

She pulled open the shop door. "Yes?"

The tiny woman—she couldn't have been more than four-foot-six or seven—gaped up at her. "*Excusez-moi.* I am wanting to speak with Aubert. Aubert Pelletier?"

Lizzie realized who the woman reminded her of: her own darling *maman.* She had similar delicate features and dark, curly hair. "I'm sorry. He…well, he sold me this place a month ago. He doesn't live here anymore."

"But…where has he gone?"

"Back to France, I think his real estate agent said."

"Back to France…" The woman's huge eyes seemed

to get even bigger as tears welled up in them. She put her hand over her soft rosebud of a mouth.

Lizzie made a snap decision. "Come in. Please."

"Oh, *non,* I am not here to bother you…"

"Please." Lizzie stepped back.

The woman gave her a wobbly smile. She brushed a tear from her eye. "You have been crying, too, eh?"

Lizzie drew in a shaky breath. "I'm Lizzie."

"And I am Colette."

Upstairs in the living room, Lizzie served coffee and fresh-baked croissants. And she kept the box of tissues handy.

"I…left Aubert two months ago." Colette dabbed at her wet eyes.

"You were living with him here?"

Colette nodded. "We met here. At the Hitching Post, down the street. I was staying at the resort, a little trip to America, to see the Wild West after a very messy divorce. That was in September of last year. He was a sad man. Trying to build a business here, longing for home. Aubert is from Paris. I'm from Lyon. Still, it was like magic with us, finding someone from home in this faraway place."

"You fell in love?"

Colette nodded. "I moved in here, with him, above his bakery. For a while, we were so happy. He wanted me to marry him. I was…reluctant. I'd just broken free of a bad relationship. I wanted to remain free."

"Oh, I know how that goes…"

Colette's big eyes were so wise right then. "You have left someone, too, I think."

"Yeah. *He* was the one who wanted to be free. But still, same result, huh?"

Colette seemed to draw herself up. "Oh, I hope not." She set down her coffee cup. "Wonderful croissants."

"Thank you."

"As good as Aubert's."

"I'm flattered. I understand he's a very talented baker."

"He is." Colette blew her delicate little nose. "And I love him. I want him. I want to *be* with him. To marry him."

Lizzie gave her a sideways look. "What about being free?"

Colette tucked the tissue into her purse and made a flicking movement of her hand, a gesture that seemed to Lizzie to be supremely French. "I don't want to be free of Aubert. I know that now. I came here today to tell him so."

"So...what will you do next?" Lizzie asked, although she'd already guessed the answer.

"Go home," said Colette. "Fly to Paris and find the man I love."

Lizzie sighed and pressed her palms to her cheeks. "Oh, now *that* is what I needed to hear."

"I *will*," said Colette, rising. "I will go, I will find my love. And I will tell him that yes, I will marry him, I *want* to marry him." Her slim shoulders drooped a little. "I only hope I am not too late."

Lizzie stood up, too. "Don't even think it," she commanded. "It's all going to work out beautifully. You'll see."

"Ah, Lizzie. You give me hope."

"He's going to be so thrilled to see you, so glad you've come back to him. I just know it. You're going to be so happy together."

They went back down the stairs. Lizzie pressed a newly printed business card into Colette's delicate hand. "Call me. Anytime you need encouragement. Don't give up."

"*Merci,* Lizzie. You, too, must keep courage in your heart. May your lover realize what a fool he's been and find his way back to you."

In the hectic days that followed, Lizzie often found herself thinking of Colette, hoping that the Frenchwoman had found her man, that Colette and Aubert were together in the city of love.

Wednesday morning, as she sipped her coffee and stood at the front window, she saw Ethan's SUV go by again. Her heart lifted—for a moment anyway.

Until he drove on past just like before, without stopping, without even slowing down.

She had started hoping. She couldn't help it. Hoping Colette's last words to her might come true. That he would see he'd been all wrong to let her go and find his way back to her. She even considered going to him, trying again to make it work between them...

But what good would that do in the end? The basic problem remained. They simply did not want the same things out of life. She'd told him she loved him, told him exactly what she wanted from him. If he changed his mind, if he decided he wanted more than just a love affair, well, he knew where to find her.

She turned from the window and went downstairs and got to work.

Working helped. It helped a lot. By the end of the day, she was worn-out. She slept deeply and without dreaming. That was a blessing. If she couldn't have Ethan, at least she didn't have to dream of him at night.

Friday morning, Colette called. It was Friday afternoon in Paris and she and Aubert were together and staying that way. Lizzie congratulated them both and thanked her for calling and letting her know.

Before they said goodbye, Colette asked if Lizzie's love had come to his senses yet. Lizzie confessed that he hadn't.

Colette said, "I know he will. I feel it in my heart."

Saturday morning, Lizzie was up at three and downstairs working. The air of the shop was filled with the sweet smell of baking.

One of her employees arrived at five and the other at six-thirty.

By eight, when they opened the doors, there was a line down the street. Lizzie stood by the door and greeted her customers. Many of them she knew. Allaire, Tori, Hayley, Shandie, Steph, Erin and Erika were all there, along with their husbands. Allaire brought her little boy and Hayley's brothers came, too. Steph and Grant brought their son and Erika brought her daughter.

There were a whole lot of Traubs. Besides Allaire and her family, Corey and Erin, Dax and Shandie and Shandie's little one, Kayla, there was also Rose. And Jackson Traub. Jackson said he was following in his brothers' and sister's footsteps, planning on moving to town.

Along with Grant and Steph, there was Elise Clifton Cates and her husband, Matt.

And more. So many more. People Lizzie recognized, some of whose names she remembered, some not. And a whole bunch of other people she'd never met before.

It seemed to Lizzie as though the whole town had turned out. Many had clipped the free-muffin coupon she'd offered in the newspaper. They got their free muffins and they bought more. They also bought bagels, fruit and cheese Danish, breads and fruit kuchen. They ordered coffee to go and coffee to stay. They filled the tables and when there were no more chairs, they took their orders and stood around the big, high-ceilinged room sipping and chatting.

Lizzie got compliments. So many. She beamed in satisfaction. Everyone loved the muffins, of course. But they all loved what she'd done to the place, too. They admired the new café lights with their blown-glass shades of swirling orange, yellow and blue, which echoed the color scheme. She'd painted two walls in sunny yellow and one in orange. And the long one behind the counter was a rich, deep burnt umber.

At waist level along each wall flowed an endless chain of mountain bluebells, hand-stenciled by Allaire. Lizzie promised everyone who asked that yes, within the week there would be Wi-Fi. They could bring their laptops, eat Mountain Bluebell muffins, drink espresso and surf the web to their hearts' content. Everyone said it was charming and homey, the kind of place you wanted to come and sit and chat for hours.

And most of her friends did just that. A lot of folks came and went, clutching bags of goodies as they rushed out the door. But Lizzie's girlfriends and their families hung around. So did Rose and Jackson. They all had second and third cups of coffee and most had more than one muffin or cinnamon roll.

By nine-fifteen, the mad rush had been handled. There was still business coming in, but the line down the street had been dealt with. Lizzie left her two employees, Rhea and Giselle, to handle the counter on their own, grabbed a vanilla latte and went to sit with her friends.

She'd just taken the chair between Allaire and Tori when Allaire elbowed her in the ribs. "Guess who?"

Corey, across the table next to Erin, said loud enough that Lizzie heard him, "And about time, too."

The little bell over the door jingled. Lizzie heard it only vaguely, like a faint echo from the real world.

She herself was somewhere else.

She was...transported. To some dreamy, impossible place.

A place where only two people existed.

Lizzie. And the tall, dark, irresistible Texan who had just come in the door.

She heard herself whisper in a voice suitable for praying, "Ethan. Oh, Ethan..."

And then he saw her—but then, how could he miss her?

She was a tall woman, after all. And somehow, without realizing she was doing it, she had risen to her feet. She kind of floated away from the table. And everyone else had moved aside—silently, it seemed to Lizzie.

There was a clear path between her and the man at the door.

"Lizzie," he said. Just that. Just her name, rough and low, with passionate intent.

And she knew then. She had no doubts. None. Not a one.

He wasn't here to wish her well, or to order his favorite strawberry-rhubarb pie. He wasn't here to support her on her opening day.

He was here for her in the truest, simplest, most basic way.

She knew it. She could feel it in her bones.

He crossed the wide plank floor in long, swift strides, stopping only inches away from her. His eyes were dark as midnight. And they were focused only on her. He spoke, his voice as husky and rough and low as it had been when he said her name at the door. "I've been by this place every day for the past week—and more than once before that."

She swallowed. Hard. "I...saw you, twice. Both times in the morning. You didn't stop. You didn't slow down."

His dark gaze searched her face. "I couldn't. I wanted..." He seemed to run out of words. But then he muttered, gruffly, "Lizzie, I was afraid..."

"Oh, Ethan..."

"I've been such a damn idiot."

As if she could deny that. "Oh, yeah, you have."

"I'm so sorry. You can't know. I'm usually smarter than this, but I guess I just got locked into a certain idea of myself. It took me way too long to see that I'm not that guy anymore. It's no fun being single, not anymore. I've been so stupid, not seeing how I love you, not admitting the truth to myself. But I know what I want now, Lizzie. I want you and me, together. I want you for my wife."

His wife. He wanted her for his wife. That was beyond huge. She really needed to say something, but all that would come out was, "Ethan..."

"Lizzie. Oh, God. Don't say it's too late."

"Ethan, I..." How to say it? How to tell him?

And right then, in the middle of her bakery on her opening day, he dropped to his knees.

Somebody gasped.

And from over near the cash register, she clearly heard Jackson Traub let out a groan. "I don't believe it." Jackson said a bad word. "He took a knee."

And he had. Right there in front of everybody, Ethan Traub was on his knees. Lizzie stared down at him and he put a hand over his heart and gazed up at her with a world of passion and longing in his eyes. It was the most perfect, beautiful, *right* moment of her life—so far.

Ethan said, "I love you, Lizzie Landry. There is no woman in the world for me but you. You're it. My answer to the big question I didn't even know I'd been asking myself until you finally got fed up with me and moved out of my house. You are the only one. I've been a fool. I know it. But if you'll only give me one more chance, I'll never be a fool again—not about what matters anyway. Not about you and me. I swear it, Lizzie. I love you and only you. And I'm willing to come here to your bakery every day for the rest of my life to get my muffins in the morning—if you'll only promise to come home to me every night."

She put her hands against her burning cheeks. "Is this… really happening?"

"Lizzie." He reached up, caught her left wrist, brought it down to him. And…there was something in his other hand. Something sparkly. "Marry me, Lizzie." He slipped a huge, gorgeous diamond onto her ring finger.

"Oh, Ethan…"

"Say yes," he pleaded.

And somehow, she did it, she managed to whisper the word that mattered most. "Yes."

"Lizzie!" He swept to his feet and he reached for her, gathering her close to him. "Aw, Lizzie…"

And he kissed her then. A beautiful, perfect, tender kiss.

And everyone in the bakery burst into wild applause.

When he lifted his head, she opened her eyes and gazed at him. And he looked…so happy. So sure. So full of joy.

She said, "I can't believe you just asked me to marry you right here in front of everyone."

He pulled her close and he whispered so only she could hear, "Remember that night you told me that someday I'd find someone special and I'd *want* to settle down?"

She sighed. "And you said you didn't do serious, that you never would."

"And then you punched me in the arm."

"Yeah, I remember that, too."

"It was a good punch. Hurt like hell. And I deserved it. I was so wrong. Because it was you, Lizzie. Even then, when I didn't have a clue. It was always you." He wrapped an arm across her shoulder and turned to all their friends and his various relatives with a big, broad smile. "Ladies and gentlemen, she said yes!"

Everyone started clapping again, even the little kids. There was whistling and a few catcalls and some more groaning from Jackson as he came to grips with the idea that another of his brothers had voluntarily surrendered to love.

Lizzie pushed Ethan into the empty seat next to Allaire. And then all her friends were up and crowding around to see the ring, to wish her well.

A few minutes later, she bent close to him and whispered, "How about a blueberry muffin?"

He gazed up at her, a killer smile curving his mouth and all the love in his heart shining in his eyes. "Blueberry. Yeah. I thought you'd never ask."

* * * * *

Don't miss
THE BABY WORE A BADGE
by Marie Ferrarella,
the next book in
MONTANA MAVERICKS:
THE TEXANS ARE COMING!
On sale August 2011.

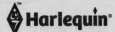

COMING NEXT MONTH

Available July 26, 2011

#2131 THE BABY WORE A BADGE
Marie Ferrarella
Montana Mavericks: The Texans are Coming!

#2132 COURTNEY'S BABY PLAN
Allison Leigh
Return to the Double C

#2133 BIG SKY BRIDE, BE MINE!
Victoria Pade
Northbridge Nuptials

#2134 THE MOMMY MIRACLE
Lilian Darcy

#2135 THE MOGUL'S MAYBE MARRIAGE
Mindy Klasky

#2136 LIAM'S PERFECT WOMAN
Beth Kery
Home to Harbor Town

SPECIAL EDITION

REQUEST YOUR FREE BOOKS!
2 FREE NOVELS PLUS 2 FREE GIFTS!

◆ Harlequin®

SPECIAL EDITION
Life, Love & Family

YES! Please send me 2 FREE Harlequin® Special Edition novels and my 2 FREE gifts (gifts are worth about $10). After receiving them, if I don't wish to receive any more books, I can return the shipping statement marked "cancel." If I don't cancel, I will receive 6 brand-new novels every month and be billed just $4.49 per book in the U.S. or $5.24 per book in Canada. That's a saving of at least 14% off the cover price! It's quite a bargain! Shipping and handling is just 50¢ per book in the U.S. and 75¢ per book in Canada.* I understand that accepting the 2 free books and gifts places me under no obligation to buy anything. I can always return a shipment and cancel at any time. Even if I never buy another book, the two free books and gifts are mine to keep forever.

235/335 HDN FEGF

Name	(PLEASE PRINT)

Address	Apt. #

City	State/Prov.	Zip/Postal Code

Signature (if under 18, a parent or guardian must sign)

Mail to the Reader Service:
IN U.S.A.: P.O. Box 1867, Buffalo, NY 14240-1867
IN CANADA: P.O. Box 609, Fort Erie, Ontario L2A 5X3

Not valid for current subscribers to Harlequin Special Edition books.

Want to try two free books from another line?
Call 1-800-873-8635 or visit www.ReaderService.com.

* Terms and prices subject to change without notice. Prices do not include applicable taxes. Sales tax applicable in N.Y. Canadian residents will be charged applicable taxes. Offer not valid in Quebec. This offer is limited to one order per household. All orders subject to credit approval. Credit or debit balances in a customer's account(s) may be offset by any other outstanding balance owed by or to the customer. Please allow 4 to 6 weeks for delivery. Offer available while quantities last.

HSE11B

*Once bitten, twice shy. That's Gabby Wade's motto—
especially when it comes to Adamson men.
And the moment she meets Jon Adamson her theory
is confirmed. But with each encounter a little* something
*sparks between them, making her wonder if she's been
too hasty to dismiss this one!*

*Enjoy this sneak peek from ONE GOOD REASON
by Sarah Mayberry, available August 2011
from Harlequin® Superromance®.*

Gabby Wade's heartbeat thumped in her ears as she marched to her office. She wanted to pretend it was because of her brisk pace returning from the file room, but she wasn't that good a liar.

Her heart was beating like a tom-tom because Jon Adamson had touched her. In a very male, very possessive way. She could still feel the heat of his big hand burning through the seat of her khakis as he'd steadied her on the ladder.

It had taken every ounce of self-control to tell him to unhand her. What she'd really wanted was to grab him by his shirt and, well, explore all those urges his touch had instantly brought to life.

While she might not like him, she was wise enough to understand that it wasn't always about liking the other person. Sometimes it was about pure animal attraction.

Refusing to think about it, she turned to work. When she'd typed in the wrong figures three times, Gabby admitted she was too tired and too distracted. Time to call it a day.

As she was leaving, she spied Jon at his workbench in the shop. His head was propped on his hand as he studied blueprints. It wasn't until she got closer that she saw his eyes were shut.

He looked oddly boyish. There was something innocent and unguarded in his expression. She felt a weakening in her resistance to him.

"Jon." She put her hand on his shoulder, intending to shake him awake. Instead, it rested there like a caress.

His eyes snapped open.

"You were asleep."

"No, I was, uh, visualizing something on this design." He gestured to the blueprint in front of him then rubbed his eyes.

That gesture dealt a bigger blow to her resistance. She realized it wasn't only animal attraction pulling them together. She took a step backward as if to get away from the knowledge.

She cleared her throat. "I'm heading off now."

He gave her a smile, and she could see his exhaustion.

"Yeah, I should, too." He stood and stretched. The hem of his T-shirt rose as he arched his back and she caught a flash of hard male belly. She looked away, but it was too late. Her mind had committed the image to permanent memory.

And suddenly she knew, for good or bad, she'd never look at Jon the same way again.

Find out what happens next in ONE GOOD REASON, available August 2011 from Harlequin® Superromance®!

Celebrating

Blaze **10** *years of*

red-hot reads

Featuring a special August author lineup of
six fan-favorite authors who have written
for Blaze™ from the beginning!

The Original Sexy Six:

Vicki Lewis Thompson
Tori Carrington
Kimberly Raye
Debbi Rawlins
Julie Leto
Jo Leigh

Pick up all six Blaze™
Special Collectors' Edition titles!

August 2011

Plus visit
HarlequinInsideRomance.com
and click on the Series Excitement Tab
for exclusive Blaze™ 10th Anniversary content!

www.Harlequin.com

SPECIAL EDITION

Life, Love, Family and Top Authors!

IN AUGUST, HARLEQUIN SPECIAL EDITION FEATURES
USA TODAY BESTSELLING AUTHORS
MARIE FERRARELLA AND *ALLISON LEIGH.*

THE BABY WORE A BADGE
BY *MARIE FERRARELLA*

The second title in the **Montana Mavericks:
The Texans Are Coming!** miniseries....

Suddenly single father Jake Castro has his hands full with
the baby he never expected—and with a beautiful young
woman too wise for her years.

COURTNEY'S BABY PLAN
BY *ALLISON LEIGH*

The third title in the **Return to the Double C** miniseries....

Tired of waiting for Mr. Right, nurse Courtney Clay takes
matters into her own hands to create the family she's
always wanted— but her surly patient may just be
the Mr. Right she's been searching for all along.

**Look for these titles and others in August 2011
from Harlequin Special Edition wherever books are sold.**

BIG SKY BRIDE, BE MINE! *(Northridge Nuptials)* by *VICTORIA PADE*
THE MOMMY MIRACLE by *LILIAN DARCY*
THE MOGUL'S MAYBE MARRIAGE by *MINDY KLASKY*
LIAM'S PERFECT WOMAN by *BETH KERY*

SEUSA0811